"KISS ME, MARGARET"

Pulling her hands forward until they touched the rock behind his shoulders, he forced her nearer. It was not at all what Margaret expected. She had thought that seducers were active, pressing their attentions on their passive, subdued victims.

But she proceeded cautiously—kissing his brow, his eyes, his cheek, but never the firm, finely drawn mouth. Yet she leaned across the last few inches separating them and pressed his lips lightly with her own.

And though she heard his breath catch in his throat and felt his hands tighten around her wrists, the greater wonder was that she should be so shaken... so eager to press not just her lips but her whole self to him.

**Winner of the
Romance Writers of America's
Golden Heart Award**

Other Regency Romances from Avon Books

TO
KISS A THIEF

KATE MOORE

AVON BOOKS ◆ NEW YORK

TO KISS A THIEF is an original publication of Avon Books. This work has never before appeared in book form. This work is a novel. Any similarity to actual persons or events is purely coincidental.

AVON BOOKS
A division of
The Hearst Corporation
1350 Avenue of the Americas
New York, New York 10019

Copyright © 1992 by Kate Moore
Published by arrangement with the author
Library of Congress Catalog Card Number: 91-92084
ISBN: 0-380-76473-3

First Avon Books Printing: January 1992

AVON TRADEMARK REG. U.S. PAT. OFF. AND IN OTHER COUNTRIES, MARCA REGISTRADA, HECHO EN U.S.A.

Printed in the U.S.A.

RA   10 9 8 7 6 5 4 3 2 1

1

A T THE SOUND of heels clicking against the flag-
stones of the terrace Margaret drew up her slip-
pered feet and pressed herself deeper into her hiding
place. She did not wish to be caught truant from the
drawing room the one evening the earl had invited
other guests to join them. The great chair's full wings
must hide her face, and its cream silk upholstery must
conceal her pale muslin should one of those passing
outside the library glance through the open windows.
She tucked the little book she had found into the folds
of her gown.

"The man's plagued with brothers!" came the old
earl's gruff voice through the window. Margaret held
her breath as he developed his favorite theme—the
obstacles to Wellington's success in Spain. "If Richard
were not so busy whoring and Henry so pathetic over
his lost wife, Arthur would get the support he needs
for this spring's campaign."

"They are a sad pair," Margaret's father agreed.

"A man should be allowed to see how his sons turn
out before he gives his title or his blunt to any of
them," replied the earl, his voice swelling with indignation. The two men came into view, and passed
the first of the library's tall windows: the Earl of Had-

1

don, tall and gaunt, Margaret's father of more modest height and substantial proportions. Margaret held herself perfectly still.

"Seeing any son inherit, however, must be preferred to seeing the title go to a nephew or cousin," her father said. In two strides the men passed from sight behind the next portion of the library wall.

"Never say you are disappointed in that girl of yours, Spencer," exclaimed the earl.

"Not for a minute," her father replied. "Apple of my eye and all. Didn't take this season, though. Speaks the plain truth, you know, no flash to catch a man's eye." They reached the second window, and there was no softening or indistinctness in her father's next words. "Her mother is very disappointed. All that fuss for nothing, you know."

"Why, Spencer, that girl of yours is a Trojan! You saw her on my roan mare yesterday. What a seat, what courage! Sensible too."

"Can't take a horse into Almack's," her father said bluntly. "Maybe if she had been a son. No fuss to getting a son off, you know." Her father's words faded as the men's steps again took them behind a portion of wall.

"Never say so," came the earl's voice. "There's nothing like town to ruin a young fool."

"The boy will come about, Edmund," said her father quietly.

"So you have been saying these two years, Spencer. You don't know what it is to have a worthless son," answered the earl. There was an interval of silence between the two men as they passed before the last window, then the earl's faint words, sad but resolute: "Well, he's no son of mine any longer."

"But you still have one son," came her father's reply. The rest of their conversation was lost in the mild evening air, and Margaret knew they had rounded the corner. She stared at the open window.

Her father's words shook her. *All that fuss for nothing.*
It had been a great fuss, preparing for her season.
Margaret and her mother had begun by studying *La
Belle Assemblée* for hours and visiting all the the neigh-
bors whose daughters had made great successes of
themselves, at least in their mothers' eyes.

They had traveled from Wynrose to Bath as often
as the weather permitted, to choose Margaret's fabrics
and stand for fittings. Her mother had insisted on one
satin and one sarsenet for balls, several crepes and
jaconets for Almack's, and a variety of figured muslins
and cambrics for morning wear, all predominantly
white of course, for what could be more elegant? Then
it had been necessary to acquire gloves and hats and
shoes, and Lady Somerley herself must have some
new finery for the season, so as not to embarrass her
daughter. Later they would shop in town for those
last touches of elegance required of a baron's only
daughter at her come-out.

For weeks as the gowns were being made, their
only topic had been the season. Her mother had never
been happier than when she spoke of London, and
she was most voluble on the subject of Margaret's
anticipated triumph, the notice Margaret would receive, the beaux who would call, the one, more distinguished than the others, who would request an
interview with the baron. Then Margaret's gowns had
begun to arrive, each to be tried on with a little ritual
of sighs and hugs and paraded before her father for
his mild "How fine you look, Margaret."

Margaret tried to return to those happy hours. She
could not remember a time when she had thought
her season would be anything other than wonderful,
for she was meant to be a heroine. She had known
it the first time she had read the story of Tom True.

Gingerly she pulled the little book she'd found from
its hiding place in the folds of her gown. The spine
was broken and some of the pages were loose, as if

whoever had owned this copy had loved it well. Inside was Tom True in his brown jacket, green cap, and green nankeen britches. With his bright eyes, his fair locks, and his hands thrust in his pockets, he looked as carefree and ready for adventure as he had always been in Margaret's youth. She smiled. It was comforting to find her hero again, for she had not seen his like in London.

She turned the page and saw Tom bidding farewell to his aged parents. His periwigged father and his mother in her panniers waved from their cottage door. The next page showed the young hero choosing two sturdy, sober youths as companions. These two, called Reason and Conscience, promised never to desert their friend, and with another turn of the page, Margaret found them introducing young Master True to Prudence.

It was Margaret's childish resemblance to this character that had prompted her father to give her the book. Prudence wore a bright blue dress, blue stockings, and black shoes with silver buckles. Glossy brown curls peeped from beneath her white cap, and frank gray eyes regarded the hero unwaveringly.

At ten Margaret had readily believed herself the fortunate heroine chosen to guide Tom True through all his adventures. At sixteen she had believed she would meet him at the very next assembly in Bath. At seventeen she had looked for her hero in the ballrooms of London. Alas, she had found no sign of him there.

Their first week in town Lady Somerley was inclined to fault Margaret's wardrobe. It had been a mistake to purchase so many items in Bath after all. They sought a reputable modiste and pressed the woman to produce a half dozen new gowns, far more costly but otherwise indistinguishable in Margaret's eyes from those she already possessed. In the second week her mother faulted the instructions she herself had given Margaret. Town ways had changed more than Lady Somerley had imagined. She consulted her friends and passed on to Margaret a bewildering and contradictory array of new strictures on appropriate topics of conversation, the use of the eyes and the fan, and all the other ways to fix a man's interest.

In the third week Lady Somerley faulted her daughter. At the kind recommendation of several mothers of acknowledged beauties, a variety of creams and ointments were applied to Margaret's face. Her diet was altered to produce a wan and delicate air. Her chestnut hair was cut in short curls. Apparently the lessons of her youth were of no use in London, so she struggled to learn a new primer. But she could discern no principles in the contradictory instructions her mother repeated. She never knew when to flutter her fan, arch an eyebrow, or toss her curls. Witty phrases tangled themselves into incomprehensible nonsense on the tip of her tongue, or she fell silent. She was to be pleasing rather than wise or good, and she could not even please her mother.

Then, at Almack's, Lady Somerley took matters into her own hands, foolishly courting Brummell's notice. "My dear Lady Somerley," the Beau replied, "if you wish your daughter to be married, you must address your remarks about her merits, if indeed she has any, to some gentleman in the market for a wife." This remark, which was widely repeated in several humiliating variations, had caused her mother such acute distress that her father had packed them off, height of the season or no, for the Earl of Haddon's country seat.

Margaret would have welcomed the change, the quiet and the pleasures of the country, but her mother had not stopped talking about her daughter's failure. Into each sympathetic ear Lady Somerley poured the story, ceaselessly asking where she had failed, what she might do, what was wrong with Margaret?

Then the old earl announced that his heir, Lord Lyndhurst, would join them for a few days. Margaret could not remember Lord Lyndhurst's face, but she recalled well that he had been one of the most intimidating of the eligible males to whom she had been introduced in the few weeks of her season. As the moment of his arrival neared, Lady Somerley's complaints diminished, and her former hints to Margaret about proper dress and manner increased until at last this evening as the party moved languidly from the dining room to the drawing room, Margaret had fled from her mother's voice, seeking the earl's library at the far end of the west wing of the hall.

The quiet library was wonderful, and Margaret would be content to linger at the Earl of Haddon's estate all summer. Though her father had often been the earl's guest for hunting, she and her mother had never come to Haddon before, the old earl being a widower and having little inclination to entertain female guests and less patience for their conversation. Her host's gruffness could not spoil her pleasure, however. At Haddon they were close enough to the Dorset coast to feel the sea's cooling breeze; the library would entertain her for weeks; and the horses, particularly the little roan mare, were all that Margaret could wish for.

And the great task of capturing a man's attention, to which she had proved so unequal, could be put off for a while. Here, Wynrose, her home, where the story of her dismal season would be told again in the drawing rooms of all her mother's friends, was so remote as to be forgotten, and London, which her mother spoke of with every breath, could be forgotten too. She could be the Margaret Somerley she had always been and not be found wanting by any man.

The April sky was pale as robins' eggs, the trees black against it when the window through which she had been staring opened a bit wider as if on its own.

A man's boot, followed by a long, well-muscled leg sheathed in buckskin, slipped over the sill, seeming disembodied in the growing darkness until above them appeared a broad shoulder and a head of fair curls. The stranger shifted his weight to the foot in the library. His face was turned from Margaret as if he were looking to see if anyone outside the library had observed his entrance. Margaret felt her mouth open in surprise, but no sound emerged. The stranger drew in his other leg and without so much as a glance around him strode to the earl's desk in the center of the long room. There he lit a lamp and from his waistcoat pocket removed a key.

In the glow of the lamp Margaret could see his face, the eyes deep-set under straight dark brows, darker than the thick curls on his forehead, the cheekbones high and the narrow-bridged nose fine, the jaw tapering to the firmly squared chin, the lips compressed, every feature golden in the lamplight. No such face had appeared before her in the ballrooms of London, and she could not help but stare. The stranger's expression was grim, but Margaret thought his eyes and mouth were made for laughing.

Then he bent away from her behind the desk, and she heard the small metallic scrape of the key thrust into a lock, the low rumble of a drawer sliding open, and the rustle of papers. He straightened and held a thick packet of papers to the lamp, unfolding it and perusing the contents.

Margaret knew she should say something. She should not watch helplessly as the stranger examined the earl's papers, but his movements were so deliberate, so sure rather than nervous or furtive, that she felt more curious than alarmed. He has a key, she told herself. He did not look up; apparently he did not expect anyone to be in the library. When he had examined the papers in the packet, he replaced them and picked up a similar one. She knew at once by a subtle change in his expression that he had found whatever it was he was looking for. Again he leaned over the drawers, opening another without the key, an unlocked drawer, she guessed. From this second drawer he took several sheets of clean paper, weighed them briefly in his hands against the first packet, folded them to match the ones he had removed, placed the altered packet in the drawer and the earl's own papers in an inner pocket of his jacket. Again Margaret heard the key turn. He blew out the lamp, rose, and turned to the window. In a minute he would be gone, as quietly and mysteriously as he had come. Prompted by her stunned conscience, Margaret bravely whispered a single word. "Thief."

The stranger whirled, and his gaze caught Margaret instantly. For a moment they regarded each other in silence. A stung look in his eyes faded so quickly, Margaret could not be sure she had seen any expression in them at all save one of cool appraisal.

"Thief?" he questioned.

She had to admit to herself that the appellation hardly fit the man standing so coolly before her, but she knew what she had seen. "You stole a packet of the Earl of Haddon's papers," she accused with more truth than eagerness.

"So it appears." He advanced toward her so that she felt ever so slightly unsettled—not exactly frightened, but wary. In the fading light she could not judge his expression, but she could feel his gaze upon her face. "Do you never doubt your own eyes?"

"Seeing is believing," she replied firmly, drawing herself up tall in the chair, sure of herself on this point at least.

"But so often we see what we think to see, rather than what really is." He moved very close to her now so that she could see nothing beyond his broad shoulders.

He was a clever thief to be sure, she thought. "You

mean to confuse me with sophistry," she retorted, holding her gaze steady under his.

"Were you never taken in by a conjurer's trick at a fair?" he asked.

"Yes, but you cannot say that what I saw here tonight was mere sleight of hand, and you cannot deny that the earl's papers are in your coat pocket." She felt, rather smugly she knew, that she had won the point.

"What do you mean to do about it?"

The question embarrassed her, for she had not thought beyond the necessity of stopping him, and now that she had, she was uncomfortably conscious that her reasons for doing so had perhaps little to do with the earl's papers.

Before she could reply, he patted his pocket and said, "Come, take them back."

She really ought to. She ought to end their whole unorthodox conversation. She, who had not been alone with any of the young men she met in London, should not prolong a tête-à-tête with a thief.

"If I take them," she offered, "no one need ever hear of this incident." She sensed rather than saw his smile. Resolutely she stood, but the long period she had spent curled in the chair made her legs a bit unsteady, so that she tottered. With the same quick deliberateness of motion that she had seen in him from the beginning, the thief caught her. He clapped a warm, firm hand across her mouth and with his other hand captured her about the waist and pulled her up against him.

At the thief's unexpected use of force, Margaret gasped. She pushed against his chest, and shook her head in a vain attempt to free her mouth from his hand. Her brief, silent struggle merely left her breathless, her arms trembling. She had not the strength to break his hold, and he had stopped her words. She drew a steadying breath and raised her gaze to his.

His eyes, blue and vivid and solemn, met hers in a look that held her more firmly than his grip about her waist or his warm hand across her mouth.

Margaret summoned all that she knew of courage and conscience and let her eyes speak, but the force of her principles seemed as weak as straw against the fire of some unshakable purpose in him.

"My girl," he whispered hoarsely, "I do not know who has greater cause to regret our meeting tonight. I do know we have tarried long enough. I must have the earl's papers, and you, alas, must come with me." Even with one hand the stranger had no difficulty restraining her movements as he removed his neck-cloth. With it he covered Margaret's mouth, muffling further protest. He swept her along to the window as if she were a mere doll in his arms, apparently indifferent as she twisted helplessly in his hold. The low sill hardly presented an obstacle as he slung her over his shoulder and stepped out into the night.

MARGARET REACHED FOR the cloth that bound her mouth, but her fingers could not loosen the knot, and her chin collided with the stranger's back, jarring her teeth. She clutched his coat to keep from being jounced senseless. She must protest, but she could not speak. She must act. No gently bred young woman should suffer herself to be carried off in the arms of a stranger, but it was impossible to determine what to do when one was being borne along at such a giddy pace and by such an odd means of conveyance. It was something like being carried by sedan-chair bearers in Bath who had suddenly gone mad and overturned their passengers. As they crossed the terrace, she willed herself to consider the practical difficulties of escaping the thief's hold.

Then they were dashing down the long steep hill which fell away from the west wing of the earl's hall, and any struggle on her part would likely send them both tumbling dangerously. She counseled herself to wait for the right moment to escape.

They reached the edge of the woods at the bottom of the hill even as she considered other ways to check their flight. The thief seemed to know exactly where they were going, and it occurred to her that he was acting according to some plan. She was not surprised when a path opened up before them in the woods. He lowered her feet to the ground and gently removed the cloth from her mouth. Before she could move an inch, his hands closed about her arms. She opened her mouth, but his words forestalled her.

"You may scream, if you like," he said, "but as a practical means of effecting an escape, I cannot recommend it. We are now quite distant from the hall." He whistled a low two-toned note, like a bird's call, and she thought she heard a horse nicker and stamp in reply. There was an answering whistle, and then her companion pulled her forward. A single long ray of light appeared to bob toward them in the darkness.

The thought that the thief might have an accomplice strengthened her resolve. She had been resisting the thief's pull on her wrist so that their arms were extended like a taut rope. As the beam of light bobbed closer, she darted forward, slackening his hold on her wrist. Instantly she twisted free and spun about, intending to slip into the brush, but branches caught at her skirts.

"Drew?" said a voice that sounded familiar.

"Here, Ned," her abductor answered. As quick as she had been, he was quicker and captured her about the waist, pulling her up against his body, and securing her flailing arms behind her back. She dug her heels into the ground, but the thin slippers slid over leaves and loose earth as the thief pushed her forward.

"What kept you?" the other man asked. "You'll have the devil's own time making it to Highcliffe before Cy does."

"So I shall," replied her companion with what she suspected was characteristic calm. In a little clearing they paused at last, Margaret quite breathless. There the other man withdrew the cover from the lantern he carried. At seeing him Margaret started, for he was one of the earl's grooms, a jolly, handsome fellow not much older than herself, with the sort of red hair one could see a long way off. As they stared at one another, the thief laughed and released Margaret. She distanced herself from him at once, but the look in his eyes persuaded her she could not escape. She paused to catch her breath and think what to do.

"Lord, Drew, what's she doing here?" asked the groom. Plainly he was as surprised to see Margaret as she to see him and much more troubled.

"I discovered too late that the library was occupied," her companion replied. "You seem to know the lady, Ned. Who is she?"

"She's Margaret Somerley," said the groom. "She's your . . . she's the old earl's guest."

The thief swore. The two men stared at each other, and Margaret thought she might laugh at their dismay. Then they laughed themselves, and, looking at her thief, Margaret decided she was right, his mouth and eyes were made for laughing. He returned her look, and his laugh faded, his expression becoming grave again.

"Well, Miss Somerley, what do you say to a moonlight ride?" As he spoke, he restored his ruined cravat to a surprising degree of neatness and intricacy.

"You don't mean to take her!" Ned exclaimed.

"Take me where?" Margaret asked.

"I can't leave her with you, Ned," said the thief, ignoring Margaret's question. "She has apparently an excess of conscience, and I don't mean for you to hang for this night's work."

Hanging. The suggestion of it sobered her, but she stood firm, refusing to shrink from her captor in spite of a very small but very sharp fear. She realized she had not felt particularly afraid of him. He had shocked her with his use of force, but her resistance to him had been a matter of affronted dignity. They had been talking, and he had used an unfair advantage, and she had been unable to reason with him. Now she considered that perhaps he had stolen something so valuable that she might be in danger because she had witnessed his crime, but she could not credit it. After all, his accomplice was not some villainous criminal, but the friendly and familiar groom of the Earl of Haddon. It was all a trick or a game, something Tom True would have dreamed up, and she had only to remind these men of their proper roles and this foolish episode would end.

She turned to the groom. "Are you going to allow this man to steal papers from your employer?"

The red-haired young man looked from her to his friend with some confusion and closed his mouth tight.

"Well, shouldn't *you* attempt to rescue me?" she asked him.

"Rescue you?" he said, as if he did not comprehend her meaning. "Oh, you mean from Drew."

Margaret felt that however patient she might be obliged to be under ordinary circumstances, she was not obliged to be patient in this one. "This is an abduction, isn't it?" she pointed out.

"Only because I forgot about you when I gave Drew the all-clear," he retorted. "You're in no danger from Drew, at least not the sort of danger you're worried about. He hasn't touched a woman in two years."

The thief named Drew laughed. "Thank you, Ned, for making Miss Somerley a gift of my ill luck as a lover. I hardly think your revelation reassures her."

"Well, she ought to see you're a gentleman. And you couldn't stop being one just because . . ."

"Is one gentleman allowed to steal from another?" asked Margaret.

"Steal? You think he stole . . ." began the groom.

"Enough," said the thief. He gave his companion a look that Margaret could only describe as a warning.

Ned shrugged and brought forward the horse he had been leading. The horse, a gray stallion as fine as any in the earl's stable, nudged the thief playfully.

"Which horse has Miss Somerley been riding?" her thief asked.

"Cinnamon." Ned named the roan mare Margaret liked so much.

"Then take Cinnamon to Upton for the night, and keep your ears open for how they take Miss Somerley's disappearance at the hall."

At the word *disappearance* Margaret glanced around for an opening in the trees, but the thief anticipated her flight and tossed her up to the gray's saddle. She dug her heels into the horse's side, leaning forward in a message of urgency the dullest nag could understand, but the great gray beneath her only flicked his ears as if to rid himself of a fly. Margaret righted herself. She might have guessed the man's horse would be as loyal as his red-haired accomplice.

"I'll see that no one knows of your involvement in this, Ned," the thief was saying.

"Don't worry about me, Drew," the other replied. "Take care of yourself with that damned Croisset."

"I mean to." The thief mounted behind Margaret. He leaned forward, stroking the horse and speaking softly. A slight touch of his knees to the horse's flanks set the animal in motion. Margaret shivered, suddenly cool in her thin muslin with her arms and throat bare, cool except for the warm proximity of the man behind her. His chest against her back, his arms on either side of her, the linen of his neckcloth against her bare shoulder—these were oddly distracting sensations, but she must not be distracted by them, for she had quite lost control of her situation. She was not Prudence, persuading Tom True to choose a wise course. She was Margaret, being carried through the dark wood farther and farther from the hall and those who would care what became of her. With her favorite mount gone her parents would probably believe she had run away. Her absence during the evening, indeed, her withdrawal from her mother ever since they had arrived at Haddon, would lend credence to the idea. She straightened and leaned forward, achieving a slight distance between them. She had to think.

"Cold?" he asked.

"No," she lied and thought he laughed.

"So you do know how to lie," he said amicably. "If it makes you less rare, it is, nevertheless, a useful accomplishment."

"It must be in your line of work," she replied, annoyed at being seen through again. The pause before he answered her was the tiniest bit too long, she thought.

"Oh, yes," he agreed, "but the trick is in knowing what to lie about. You, it seems, know the London lie—that is, you know how to deny what is perfectly obvious to your companion in order that both may be saved from embarrassment." He paused, and in a changed voice said, "My Lord Leadfeet, nothing would please me more than to dance with you, but the room is so warm, do you think you might bring me some refreshment first? Lady Loosetongue, so good to see you again."

Margaret had to laugh at his mimicry, but it confused her too, for he was talking as if they were partners in a ballroom. She could not reconcile his light words with his acts. Her mother had certainly never advised her on the subject of polite discourse with a kidnapper.

She shook herself, not deigning to answer him, and stared ahead. At the very next opening she would slip from the horse. Though her pale gown must show against the black brush and tree trunks, this time she was sure she could lose her abductor. Then she would simply climb a tree and wait for dawn. At first light she would find her way back to the hall. Then she would show the earl the drawer that had been opened. However angered the thief might be at her escape, he was unlikely to pursue her for long, because he had miles to go to keep the appointment the red-haired groom had mentioned. She tensed for the effort she must make.

Just as she saw a widening in the path ahead, he encircled her ribs with one strong arm and pulled her firmly against him.

"Oh," she exclaimed. Once again he had anticipated her actions and thwarted her. What was she to do?

"You know," he said, "I am inclined to think that my removing you from the hall should be considered a rescue rather than an abduction."

"A rescue?" She could not think as clearly as she wished to, conscious as she was of his fingers over her ribs and the way the horse's easy movement caused her bare arm to slide up and down against the silk of his waistcoat. "Did you think I was a prisoner there?"

"What else could explain it? A pretty girl, immured in a library in the country when there must be three balls and a Venetian breakfast to attend in London. Confess, I did rescue you—from boredom."

"No," she said, momentarily disconcerted by his phrase "pretty girl." He was offering Spanish coin, of course. "No, not from boredom, from my own thoughts perhaps."

He laughed at that, and his breath stirred her hair. "You *are* an honest girl, Meg Somerley."

"Miss Somerley to you," she said.

"Never Meg?"

"Never."

"But tonight you must be Meg, for you are having the adventure Margaret Somerley merely dreams of."

It was a conjecture so accurate and penetrating that

she wondered if he had seen the little book in her lap, had guessed her dreams.

They had come to the edge of the wood, and the horse lunged up a short embankment to a road bathed in the light of a quarter moon rising to their left. The horse pranced and sidled, but her companion stilled the powerful animal and held him lightly in check.

"Now, Miss Somerley," he said, the playfulness gone from his voice, "you must swear not to make any attempts to escape before we reach Highcliffe."

Margaret said nothing. She had determined on no safe means of escape, yet he seemed to anticipate her every thought.

"Swear it," he insisted. "I mean to give Phantom his head, and it would likely cost you your pretty neck to slip from him along the road."

"I swear," she said with grudging acquiescence.

"Not good enough, my girl."

Margaret remained stubbornly silent. The horse shifted restlessly beneath them, and the movement rocked Margaret's body against the thief's from knee to shoulder. The words she had heard earlier in the wood came back to puzzle her. *He hasn't touched a woman in two years.* He certainly had touched her.

"I swear to make no attempt to escape before Highcliffe."

"Good," he said. He released his hold on her ribs, and she felt him stretch and twist behind her. In a moment he had draped his jacket about her shoulders, the blue superfine warm and softer than she thought a man's garment would be, the papers in the inner pocket heavy against her arm.

"It is not me you are taking. It is these papers. Could you not leave me behind?"

"You underestimate yourself, Meg. It gives me no pleasure at all to carry off the earl's papers."

Margaret made no reply. It was plain he meant to offer her flattery, not reason.

"Slip your arms into the sleeves," he commanded. When she complied, he tightened his hold on her waist once more. With less impatience he continued, "In Highcliffe there is a kind soul who will keep you for the night and restore you to your family in the morning." He pressed his knees lightly against the horse's sides, and, thus encouraged, Phantom broke into an easy canter.

Margaret knew at once that her promise not to escape was superfluous. She could not escape now. The rider at her back urged and checked, encouraged and steadied the animal so that they seemed to fly along, man and stallion apparently relishing the risks they were taking. In the movement of the man's thigh against her own, in the steady arms about her, and in the voice at her ear, Margaret felt every message of rider to horse, and always Phantom responded. They passed through startling alterations of light and shadow along the road, crossed glittering creeks, and flew by oddly contorted black shapes which, Margaret believed, must be gorse bushes by day.

Though she was insensible of anything so ordinary and rational as thought, Margaret felt she knew the stranger's mind as she had when she first looked into his eyes. From his very proximity she seemed to catch his thoughts, his urgency and intensity, his reckless courage. Every feeling of the sort was absurd, for how could she have the least idea of his mind when they had not exchanged a word for miles? Yet her body could not help but move with his in the impatient, drumming rhythm of the canter.

When at last they left the road for the merest lane, she was embarrassed to discover how tightly she was pressed against him and would have pulled forward at once, but his arm held her. He halted Phantom and dismounted.

"Miss Somerley," he said, holding up his arms to her. She hesitated only long enough to think herself foolish, for she had already allowed greater intimacies between them. Again she felt the strength in his arms and shoulders. He took her by the hand and began walking at once. It was this unwavering advance of his, rather than their actual speed, that gave Margaret a sense of his haste.

The lane was nearly overgrown with trees and tangled vines so that the moonlight scarcely penetrated, but a turn or two brought a light in view and a fenced garden before a snug cottage. A path to their right led to a modest stable toward which Phantom moved eagerly, showing all the impatience of a horse who has done well and knows he deserves the rewards and comforts of the stall. The thief lifted the latch, allowing the heavy door to swing open. The stable was lit as if they were expected, and a horse in one of the stalls nickered at their entrance.

The thief turned to Margaret. "Whatever you think of me, Miss Somerley, you must agree that Phantom deserves my attentions for his efforts tonight. I must rely on you to remain where you are for a few minutes. Your adventure is nearly at an end. Can you be patient a while longer?"

Margaret shook her head. She did not trust herself to speak.

"I thought not," he said. In an instant he stripped the linen from his neck and bound her hands. He set her up on a partition between the stalls and, his hands still on her waist, looked directly into her eyes. "You *will* wait for me."

She looked away, but soon turned back to watch him. She could not help but admire the quickness and sureness of his motions, the care and skill of his attentions to the horse. He talked to the horse, praising and teasing, and she felt the calming influence of his voice. The thought occurred to her that she had not watched a man so closely before. When he spoke, assuring her that his tasks were nearly complete, she shifted her weight upon her narrow perch and looked down at her bound hands. The movement brought the papers in his jacket up against her ribs. Really she was behaving witlessly. She ought not to have been staring, ought not to have been admiring the appearance and strength of a thief. If she could not escape, perhaps she could at least hide the earl's papers.

But the thief turned from his horse and reached to lift Margaret down. He pulled her after him, though her strides could hardly match his long, quick ones. At the cottage he called, "Humphrey, where are you, man?"

They entered a low-ceilinged parlor, the striking feature of which was stacks and stacks of books, like staircases about to topple, so many that Margaret and the thief had to pick their way with care. Before the fire, like an island in the chaos, was a conspicuously empty wing chair, with a table anchored to one side.

"Humphrey," her companion called again, but received no answer. He led her through the maze of stacks to a door in the far wall of the parlor, and Margaret sent a pile crashing to the floor, taking two others with it so that in one corner there was now a heap of books.

"Don't worry," her captor assured her, "Humphrey will not notice for weeks." A hall at the rear of the cottage led them to a room, black except for the patch of moonlight admitted by a window. The thief found a tinderbox in the dark and lit two candles, revealing a spare order in startling contrast to the main parlor. He led her to the bed, bade her be seated, and released her hands.

"It seems your adventure continues," he said as he removed a watch from his waistcoat pocket and glanced at it. Margaret studied him further, this thief named Drew. She had kept herself from saying his name, for she meant not to be on terms of any familiarity with such a man. She was beginning to recognize the cold alteration in his voice and features whenever he spoke of the meeting toward which he was hurrying.

"There are a few changes I must make; let us hope Humphrey returns," he concluded in the same brusque tone. He closed the door of the small room and began to unbutton his waistcoat before her startled eyes.

"My girl," he warned, a sudden smile lighting his eyes, "if your sensibilities are at all delicate, you would do well to take a book from that shelf and peruse it earnestly for the next few minutes." Margaret turned to a shelf above the bed and snatched the volume on the end. To her dismay it proved to be a work in Latin, but she held the slim volume before her burning face and worked at the lines.

"Do you have a taste for Horace, Miss Somerley?" he asked a few minutes later. She made the mistake then of dropping the book to her lap and looking at him as he tucked the tails of a fresh shirt into his inexpressibles.

"Perhaps I ought to wait for you in the other room," she said, wishing her bright cheeks did not reveal her embarrassment so plainly.

"Alas, Miss Somerley, I cannot trust you to remain there, can I?" She shook her head, and he went on, "Then I recommend 'Ode to a Debutante,' page nineteen."

Margaret turned to it. Without looking up again she said, "This is not your home, is it." There was a pause in which she could hear the little indefinite rustle of clothes that meant he continued to move inexorably toward his objective.

"No, it is not," he answered.

"But these are your books?" she persisted. The book had opened so readily to the page he recom-

mended that she could not doubt his familiarity with
the volume.

"Yes," came the reply. "And that is my bed, Miss
Somerley."

She looked up then. "You say that merely to disconcert me," she began, and stopped at the sight of
him. He had brushed his hair forward in a style she
had often seen in London and had somehow dark-
ened the color, subdued the gold of it to a pale brown.
The coat he now wore was bottle-green and cut
differently, to exaggerate the contrast between the
broad shoulders and narrow waist. He had added
fobs and rings that made him look quite the exquisite.
The transformation was surprisingly complete, her
teasing companion as thoroughly obscured in the
haughty figure before her as if he had donned a mask
and domino.

She looked away. She had meant to tell him he was
an uncommon thief, but now it appeared he would
steal anything. She gazed at a case on the lowboy in
which a tangle of jewels sparkled.

"I meant to leave you with Humphrey, who is as
kind as he is old," he said, and his words recalled
her to her own awkward position. "But it seems Humphrey has been called away, or more likely wandered
away, on business of his own; thus you must continue
with me." He pulled her to her feet and removed the
book from her unresisting fingers.

"You could not trust me to wait here? We are far
from the hall." It was reasonable and sensible to ask,
and of course she wanted him to leave her behind so
that she might escape and alert the earl. So she held
herself perfectly still, allowing her fingertips to rest
lightly on his, meeting his clear gaze steadily. She felt
an unaccustomed tautness in her body as she waited
for his decision.

He studied her for a long moment; then, as certainly
as if he had spoken, Margaret knew he had decided

to take her with him. The change was in his eyes, and Margaret, who had sided with Prudence and Reason and Conscience all her life, knew that he had discarded the advice of such wise companions, had decided to take her because he wanted to. She dropped her gaze from his lest he should discern the perfectly unreasonable thrill that knowledge gave her.

"You would not wish to miss the end of your adventure, would you?" he asked lightly. "But you must not appear as Margaret Somerley in my company tonight."

She allowed him to remove the borrowed jacket, but when he again put the earl's papers securely in an inner pocket and tossed the first jacket aside, a pang of conscience made her appeal to him once more.

"Must you do this thing?"

"I must." He studied Margaret with a critical air. "No doubt your mother selected this gown," he said softly. "And we've no modiste to turn to." Margaret felt the briefest twinge of resentment at her mother's taste. Then he reached for her. She retreated, and the backs of her knees collided with the hard edge of the bed. In one of his quick, startling moves, he slid the tiny sleeves off her shoulders so that her chest and neck were suddenly more exposed than her mother could have approved of.

"No," she protested, hugging her shoulders, pushing against his hands, trying to restore the modesty of her neckline.

"These bows must go," he said, ignoring her attempts to right the gown. "Too demure by half for the company we'll be keeping".

Ruthlessly he plucked a row of corded ivory bows from each sleeve. Margaret pulled the poor bare puffs of muslin back up over her shoulders, but his hands met hers and stilled them. His thumbs lightly traced the line of bone from her shoulders to the hollows of her throat. She stared at him, appalled and fascinated.

"You miss your finery?" he asked abruptly. "No matter. You need another sort of ornament for your disguise."

From the sparkling array in the case on the lowboy, he drew a strand of sapphires and fastened it about her neck, his fingers tangling briefly in her curls.

"A reward for your courage," he said. She thought: How carelessly he takes and gives.

"There," he whispered, turning her so that she could look in the mirror, "Margaret Somerley becomes . . . Meg Summers." For an astonished instant Margaret gaped at her own appearance, the tumbled chestnut curls, the wide eyes more black than gray in the dim light, the flash of jewels above the white swell of her breasts.

Then her gaze met his in the mirror. He grinned. "If anyone asks where you've come from, you may say that you just left my bed."

3

ONCE MORE THEY hurried through the night. The cottage, which had seemed so remote, proved to be just steps from the main thoroughfare of a coastal village. As they emerged from a wooded path, the sea lay to their left with a stripe of moonlight on it like a glittering extension of the street. To their right shops lined the steep ascent to an inn that clearly served as a coaching stop, for even as they moved toward it Margaret heard the guard's blast on his yard of tin and saw the stage pull in.

As they entered the inn yard, the ordinary and familiar bustle of stableboys attending horses and weary travelers descending from the coach had the effect of rousing Margaret as if from a daydream. The world of ordinary action, which had seemed so remote since the thief had carried her off, now appeared accessible. She did not doubt that the unknown Humphrey would restore her to her family as the thief said, but surely here *she* could find someone kind enough to help her. Her thief appeared to be intent on his own errand and for the moment unaware of her on his arm. She had only to approach some reasonable person and explain who she was. But no one seemed to remark them. Margaret caught no one's eye.

When they entered the inn itself, her sense of familiar and comfortable surroundings was immediately dispelled. Her parents patronized only the most respectable posting houses on the Bath road, establishments that catered to the quality, to whose proprietors Margaret's father was well-known. How easy to explain her situation in one of them, how impossible here. The main taproom was plainly visible as she and the thief stood in the entry, waiting for the host to serve them. The room was dim, and a haze of pipe smoke drifted sluggishly on currents stirred by the movement of the waiters. The sober faces at the ends of the pipes appeared as unalterable as the carvings in the heavy paneling. To Margaret the inhabitants seemed not precisely evil but peculiarly indifferent. She doubted they could be moved to anything stronger than idle curiosity. She could hardly appeal to one of these.

She turned to the innkeeper, whose professional cheer and white apron made him seem a more likely rescuer, but he had eyes only for her foppishly dressed companion. She did not receive the least deference from him, and suddenly she realized the effect of her altered appearance. The borrowed cloak did little to conceal her bedraggled state; her arrival unattended by an abigail hardly suggested that she was a lady of quality. To convince anyone that she was a lady, let alone a baron's daughter, would be impossible. Her thief had not asked for any further promises from her, and now she understood why. She felt her cheeks burn, but she lifted her chin and looked disdainfully upon the innkeeper. She averted her gaze from the thief, but he stayed her in the hall some steps behind their host.

"Would you believe I did it to protect you?" he

asked softly, as if he had read her discomfort and embarrassment. She refused to answer. "No one must ever know Margaret Somerley was here; no one must ever connect you with me."

The smiling proprietor had stopped and with a flourish indicated a door near the end of the hall. When he moved to open it, the thief stopped him, offering a coin. The man's hand closed over the gold, and he bowed and left them.

In another of his swift, unexpected moves the thief encircled Margaret's waist with one arm and pulled her against his side. He tilted her chin up, compelling her to look at him. "Now, Meg Summers," he whispered, giving her the name he had invented. "Croisset must never guess who you are, so keep silent and lean against me, and I warn you, lie if you must, for he is a dangerous man." His gaze held hers, and she knew he waited for her to acknowledge that she understood. Harsh laughter burst from the taproom behind them, followed by the scrape of chairs against the floor, shouts, and jeers. In these surroundings who could she trust but her thief? Reluctantly she nodded her compliance, and they entered the parlor.

At a long table lit by a great branch of candles sat an enormous man before whom were several platters, empty except for streaks of sauce and piles of bones. Margaret's first thought was of the prince, for the man's girth was as great or greater than the regent's, and the room was uncomfortably warm, like all the rooms in Carlton House. Yet this man had none of the prince's amiability about him. His complexion was mottled, and the skin appeared like a sausage casing stretched taut over the folds of flesh. It was not a skin in which a man could be comfortable. His unblinking gaze suggested a snake's readiness to strike. Croisset's look told her he would never forget her face, and under that gaze she could not resent the thief's arm about her waist.

"So we meet at last. You are more than prompt, my lord," the enormous man said to her companion in a thin nasal voice which was at odds with his size. "It is well—" He paused. "—but you bring a woman."

"A necessary convenience, merely," the thief replied in a voice Margaret hardly recognized as his. She wondered at the title with which he had been addressed, but the pressure of his hand at her side warned her to show no surprise.

"Perhaps she could wait for you elsewhere while we talk," suggested the other with a careless wave of his hand.

"In this neighborhood there is no suitable location where a prize of her delicacy might be left alone, Croisset. I do not share what is mine." He led Margaret to a bench built into an alcove. Then he removed their cloaks and settled Margaret next to him as if he were making the most ordinary of visits.

"You are not as I imagined, my lord," said Croisset when they were seated. Again Margaret wondered at the title. Who was the man at her side? Was he lying to her or to Croisset?

"I did not think you fanciful, Croisset," he replied.

"You are more handsome, more the ladies' man than you are reported to be, I think," continued the other, looking pointedly at Margaret.

"As I said, a necessary convenience."

"But such an innocent one." Margaret could not look away from the man's stare until she felt her thief's hand once more under her chin, tilting her face toward his.

"Innocence is a charming quality, don't you think, Croisset?" he said, looking at Margaret. "Usually overpriced, but with this one, no." He stroked Margaret's cheek with his thumb. Her skin tingled and she felt the heat of the blush his touch evoked. "Did you wish to discuss her charms—I assure you she has many—or must we turn at once to the more pressing business of the evening?" He shifted his gaze back to Croisset, and there was a pause. Margaret willed her cheeks to cool, knowing the big man was deciding whether to accept her presence or not.

At last he said, "So you have brought the information we wished?"

"Of course," her companion replied, with a languid calm that Margaret could see was maddening to the other man.

"You have the numbers, dates, objectives?"

"You doubt me, Croisset? My lord Haddon is the most trusted of Wellington's supporters. While others receive only fragments of plans, Haddon has the key to the whole, that he might influence those in our government who are reluctant to supply the army's needs."

"Indeed, the information from your source has always been reliable."

"More than reliable, Croisset—and perhaps, at this time, it is invaluable as well."

"Invaluable, my lord? I thought we had agreed on a generous price." With that Margaret stiffened in the circle of her companion's arm. She understood at last and too well her thief's aim. She should have realized at the hall that the earl's papers would contain information about Wellington's plans, and she should have acted to see that the papers never left the library. Words had been far too weak to stop the thief.

"After Moscow your emperor's fortunes are not what they were; this spring's campaign is perhaps critical," her companion suggested, his hold on her as firm as ever.

Again Croisset's black eyes glittered menacingly. "The emperor will prevail," he asserted.

"Then no price will seem too much, I think, to the men who mean to rule Europe." At this Margaret felt her throat tighten.

"Alas, my lord, I am merely the emperor's courier and cannot pay more than the agreed-upon sum."

"Then our dealings are at an end, Croisset," said the thief. "You will excuse us." He stood, drawing Margaret up after him.

"My lord," said the other quickly, "if it were a simple matter, I could perhaps accommodate you. Perhaps an additional five thousand pounds?" he added.

"Really, Croisset, you underestimate the value of my information." In the pause that followed this remark the thief put Margaret's cloak gently about her shoulders.

"My lord, perhaps it was unwise of you to keep this engagement. In this neighborhood a man of your lordship's wealth presents an irresistible temptation to thieves. One could, perhaps, arrange to have your information for nothing."

"I think one will not, however, for one has spent months cultivating me as a source. One would have to begin the process again, a delay the emperor would not tolerate. And, if I believed one might try such a thing," he said, moving slowly toward the long table, "it would be easy to destroy the information here and now." With a sudden quickness and grace, the thief drew the papers from his pocket and held them over the flame of a candle so that the edges began to blacken. Croisset's protest was an inarticulate cry at which the thief removed the papers from the flame without apparent haste.

"My lord," said Croisset, regaining his calm, "if you wish to haggle like a shopkeeper over the price of your wares, you must see the Viper. Only he has the authority to pay you a larger sum."

"Very well, Croisset, then I shall see him," the thief replied, returning the papers to an inner pocket.

"Ah, but he is in Portugal, my lord," came the smug reply.

The thief did not answer, but Margaret felt him give the slightest start.

"Perhaps you shall accept what I have to offer after all," Croisset concluded.

"If I do, you mean to take the information to the Viper yourself? You have a ship waiting?" His tone was merely curious, but Margaret felt the tension gathering in him.

"I do."

"Then I have a mind to take your place, Croisset. May not one courier deliver a message as well as another?"

"You are unprepared for such a journey, my lord."

"One may make purchases."

"And the young woman? It is hardly a journey on which to take such a delicate morsel."

"Some men, Croisset, travel with their own sheets, not trusting every innkeeper along the way to be as fastidious as they themselves are. Should I take less care about what I put between my sheets? My taste in such matters is particular."

There was a pause as the two men regarded each other. "Very well, my lord," said Croisset with an unpleasant agreeableness.

The proprietor was summoned, and hastened to do his large guest's bidding. Margaret was stunned. Her thief could not mean to take her to Portugal to deliver the army's plans into the hands of the French. He was going to return her to Humphrey's cottage. Surely.

She considered running to the taproom, but the denizens of that place would hardly believe that two such gentlemen as these appeared to be—the London dandy and the fat merchant—meant to betray their country. She could perhaps make use of some womanly excuse to leave the room, but her thief would not be deceived by such a ruse. She could kick and scream, but if she aroused Croisset's suspicions would he not kill them both? He had already threatened her companion's life. The man at her side was not Tom True, but if ever a man needed prudent counsel, he did.

"My lord," she ventured, using the title Croisset had, "is it prudent to undertake such a journey in haste?"

He turned her toward him so that they stood face-to-face, a little in the shadows, beyond the light of Croisset's candles. She felt the impatience in him, the restrained force, and willed herself to remain steady in the face of it.

"Readiness to seize the prize is not haste," he replied. He put a finger to her lips as if to silence her, but she pushed it aside.

"Is it readiness to go so unprovided into danger?" she whispered.

"Is readiness in things or in the will?" he asked. Tom True had never spoken so; the hero had always listened to Prudence, altered his course, avoided danger. This man, quick and bright as a flame, meant to plunge them headlong into danger.

Their talk had come to just this unprofitable point when the proprietor returned, announcing that Mr. Crossey's carriage was waiting. Their party moved at once down the hall toward the entrance to the inn. When they came in view of the taproom, its stolid inhabitants, who had appeared so cold to Margaret earlier, cheered and toasted Croisset, inviting him to tip a cup with them. Outside, a great black traveling chaise waited with two stableboys at the horses' heads and two men on the box, apparently servants of Croisset though not in livery. Croisset was assisted into his carriage by another man at the chaise door and the innkeeper himself. The carriage tipped precariously as he put his weight upon the first step, and righted itself as he settled inside. Then Margaret was handed up by the proprietor, and the thief climbed in after her, all in a minute's time.

Though the carriage was clearly designed for Croisset, there was no room to spare and Margaret could not move without touching the man across from her or the man at her side. Escape now seemed to call for some action on a scale quite out of her experience. Her throat ached with sobs she must not release, and in the close confines of the carriage she seemed to choke on the odors of sweat and onions and wine.

The driver did not spare the whip, and after but a short interval of swaying and bouncing, the chaise turned from the main road down a lane toward the sea. Suddenly Croisset pounded the roof with his hand, and they stopped. When the clop and rattle of their mode of travel faded in her ears, Margaret could hear the hiss of waves upon the shore, and the sound of pebbles tumbling over one another as the breakers rolled them. The thief opened the chaise door, let down the steps, and handed Margaret out, keeping a grip on her arm. Margaret breathed deeply of the damp, fresh air. They had halted before a wood, which was revealed by the moon, more than halfway toward setting. Croisset's quick orders to the two servants on the box brought one of them to his assistance and sent the other scurrying ahead with a lantern.

"You still wish to meet the Viper, my lord?" Croisset asked when he had stepped down. "You do not wish to accept the sum I offer?"

"You need only to inform me how I may find this Viper, Croisset," came the reply.

"Ah, my lord, the Viper will find you. His messengers will meet your ship."

Croisset waved his hand in a gesture that might have been polite except for a certain sinister cast of his features in the moonlight, and Margaret began to descend the path taken by the servant with the lantern. The path was scarcely wide enough for her and switched back and forth sharply, making their descent quite steep. Behind her she could hear the thief, quiet and sure in his steps, and behind him Croisset, breathing loudly from his exertions and brushing the branches along the path with a noisy rustle like a dog pursuing a scent through the undergrowth. At a turning in the path where it nearly doubled back upon itself, the thief caught her arm and whispered, "Not a sound now, Meg, no matter what you hear."

He released her arm, and there was an ominous crack of a dry branch breaking. Even as she identified it in her mind, she heard a second sound which she could not identify, a sound like a bucket hitting the sides of a deep well, and a third sound, like a great bellows slowly settling. Thus, before she turned, she knew Croisset had been felled. Relief made her knees weak; her thief did not mean to go to Portugal after all. The servant ahead of them had halted, too and peered back at her, lifting his lantern high. Of the thief there was no sign.

"*Monsieur?*" called the servant hesitantly.

"I think Mr. Croisset has fallen," said Margaret.

The servant looked at her suspiciously as if he thought her words a trick. Margaret backed against the bushes as he made his way gingerly past her, repeating, "*Monsieur?*"

She held her breath, wondering where her thief was and what he meant to do. When the servant reached the turn in the path, she heard a thud and the merest squeal as if some animal's cry had been cut off before it could escape the throat from which it came, then a rustling of leaves and a tumbling of dirt and rock and then silence. She waited. Another breathless moment passed before her thief appeared with the lantern and a fat purse. His coat and breeches showed no signs of what must have been a struggle in the grass.

"Croisset and his henchman are sleeping, Meg,"

he said. "We need not fear that they will plot against us with the captain of this vessel."

"But surely you do not mean to go to Portugal now?"

"But I do," he answered. "I confess it was not my plan, but 'tis a better one."

"Then I must leave you," she said, backing away, hopelessly trapped on the narrow path between the approaching dinghy and the determined man before her.

"Ah, but I cannot let you go," he said, catching her hand and pulling her with him along the path. "Even if our sleeping friends did not wake to do you harm, there is no safety for one like you along this coast."

When they reached the bottom of the path, the dinghy touched the pebbled shore, crunching rocks and sand. The two men inside bounded over the gunwales and rapidly pulled the boat up where the surf could not dislodge it. The taller of these began to speak in French, not the French that Margaret had learned from her governess, but a rapid, peculiarly accented French full of terms Margaret had never heard. She knew just enough to understand that her companion was once again lying. He seemed to know the peculiar argot of the sailors, and when he drew glittering coins from the fat purse, she knew his lies would be accepted. She was handed into the boat, and sat upon a damp bench, pulling her cloak about her.

The brawny sailors in their soft caps pushed the boat into the surf and again took up the oars. The small craft dipped and slapped over the breakers toward a larger boat anchored in the bay. This was a vessel unlike any Margaret had ever seen, with a high-pointed prow, bright with stripes of red and yellow and blue, the colors vivid even in the moonlight. There was a single tall mast amidships before a boxlike cabin over which extended a long boom. When their dinghy pulled alongside the larger vessel, they were accosted in an unfamiliar tongue by a man Margaret took to be the captain. Again her companion spoke with languid assurance; again a glitter of gold gained compliance.

Once they were aboard, her thief led her to the central cabin, and they descended two steps to an inner door, which he opened, revealing a compartment apparently prepared for Croisset himself with a wide berth built into one wall, a lamp and chest, and other necessary accoutrements.

"Croisset meant to be comfortable, I see," he said. "I hope you will make yourself so in his stead, Meg Summers." She thought he waited for some sign of approval from her, but she felt only sobs welling up irresistibly inside her so that she could barely speak. As she did not wish to cry before him, she turned and took hold of the door handle. Only one word came to mind.

"Traitor," she said. Though it was no more than a whisper, she thought he flinched at it. She slammed the door as hard as she could, and it banged shut in a very satisfactory way. But when she looked to lock it, there was no key. A glance around the narrow cabin in which she was to make herself comfortable confirmed that she had no means of escape. Since he had carried her from the earl's library—how many hours ago?—she had been telling herself she should escape at the very next chance. Now no further chances would come. Through delay and hesitation she had allowed herself to become party to the betrayal of her country. She stood very still as the tears of weariness, frustration, and loss came at last. The ship lurched forward, and she stumbled into the berth and curled up in her cape, and very soon Margaret Somerley slept.

* * *

For a few minutes there was a bustle on the deck as all hands worked to trim the sails and get the ship underway. The young man in the green coat observed it all quite carefully. When they reached open sea and the breeze picked up, he made his way around coiled lines and nets and strings of cork and wood, away from the steersman to the prow of the boat. He leaned over the side and drew from an inner pocket a thick bundle of papers. These he unfolded and tore to pieces, allowing the white fragments to fall like leaves shaken loose in a gale. They drifted down to the inky waters and disappeared one by one in the vast blackness of the sea.

4

MARGARET WOKE TO strange sounds, not the birds or horses or dogs of Wynrose, nor the rustle of maids' skirts outside her door or the clatter of wheels outside her window in London, but to creaks and groans and sudden, sharp snaps, and a whistle of wind above her and somewhere below her a whispering rush of movement. The movement was a slow, rolling rise, a trembling pause, and a swift, sliding descent. She opened her eyes. Above her were the rough beams of the cabin to which she had been led late the night before. It was impossible that she should be here, yet here she was.

The lamp no longer burned, but a sort of gray daylight entering from two small windows illuminated the narrow compartment, only as wide again as the berth on which she lay. Against the wall opposite the door was a stand with a pitcher and basin set into holes in the top to keep them steady. Across from her were a low chest and a commode and above them several hooks on one of which she saw the thief's greatcoat and on another her cape, the cape she had been wearing when she had curled up on the berth. She felt the rough blanket that lay over her. He had entered the room as she slept, had done this simple thing for her comfort. At the thought of how he might have looked at her, at how he might have touched her, she sat up abruptly, flung off the blanket, and swung her feet over the side of the bed. Where had her slippers gone?

In her agitation she wished to move, but though the berth was wide enough for Croisset, the confines of the narrow cabin allowed her no more than a few lurching steps in either direction. How very foolish she had been in all that had to do with her thief and how selfish as well. What were her parents enduring in her absence? She had hardly spared a thought for them during the adventures of the evening before, but by now they must be distressed at her disappearance. Would they believe she had run away? Her father would be very hurt if he thought so, but how could they guess that she had been abducted? Her mother would consider only the embarrassment to the family before the Earl of Haddon and would even now be apologizing for Margaret's rudeness or lamenting Margaret's lost opportunity to meet the earl's son. At the disloyal thought, a recollection came to contradict it, a memory of her mother sitting beside her after she had broken her arm riding a forbidden colt. There had been no blame in her mother's words or looks, only comfort and reassurance. How had she come to doubt her mother so in just a few short weeks in London?

There was a knock on the door. She felt unprepared to meet him, but there was certainly no place to hide in the cramped cabin. "Come in," she said.

The handle turned and the door swung toward her. Her thief stood on the threshold with a rough wooden tray. A stirring of the air in the room brought her the smell of bread and strong coffee, and she was at once ravenous, cold, and conscious of all the needs of her body. It would be sensible, she knew, to accept the comforts and necessities the thief offered, but how

could she? Her parents must fear dangers and discomforts which she had not the merit of suffering.

He stepped forward, and she stepped back. A
pained look crossed his face. "Last night," he said,
"you advised me not to go unprovided into danger.
This morning, let me return the favor." He set the
tray on the bed, turned, and was gone, and Margaret
knew a moment of regret.

In the end, she did what she must, and settled
herself on the berth with the tray before her and the
blanket about her shoulders. A little curl of steam still
rose from the coffee. With a sigh she took the heavy
cup and sipped the hot liquid. From above she heard
muffled shouts and footsteps, and the regular creaks
and groans of wood and rope, and the flutter and
snap of canvas. Was he up there or in some other
cabin below? She resolved to remain in the cabin, to
avoid him in thought as well as in person.

It was a resolution more easily made than kept, for
during the long day she could not but reflect on the
events that had brought her to such a pass. Try as
she might to condemn her companion entirely, she
could not escape the thought that some of the blame
was hers. Surely she could have stopped him somehow.

With the gray light of a second morning, she woke
to her duty. The only right action in her situation
would be to stop the thief from selling secrets to the
French and to escape as soon as she reached Portugal
to return to England, however unwelcome she might
be there when her adventure was known. She would
not waste another day in thought.

After she had fortified herself with bread and coffee, she attempted to put to rights her rumpled person. There was no mirror to guide her efforts, but she
brushed and shook her skirts and ran her fingers
through her hair. The results could hardly be ac-
ceptable to her mother. Indeed she laughed ruefully

to herself; her mother would be horrified at the limp,
soiled muslin. She had pulled her cape from the hook
when she stopped to consider her stockinged feet.
Then she saw that her captor's coat had disappeared
in the night. When had he come? And why? She
turned to the door. Beside it were her kid slippers,
fresh and clean, though she knew they must have
been quite dirty when she had come aboard. She
stepped into them, pulled her cape tightly about her,
and opened the door.

Then she could see other doors and steps leading
to the hold and to the deck. She chose the latter,
ascending to the deck, stopped momentarily by dazzling light that brought tears to her eyes. Shading her
eyes with her hand, she looked about. Two sailors
regarded her with leering interest, and she turned
and made her way over ropes and nets to the bow of
the boat. Light bounced off the water in blinding sparkles. The sea itself was a deep purple, almost black,
except for the frothy caps of the waves. For some
minutes she watched its changing surface with no
other thought than how beautiful it was. But the
breeze whipped at her skirts, chilling her so that she
turned away from the water to find herself face-to-
face with her mysterious companion.

He sat with his back to the cabin, his legs stretched
lazily in the sun, and the very ease of his manner
fired Margaret's determination to do battle with him.

"Care to join me, Miss Somerley?" he asked. "It's
quite a bit warmer here out of the wind." He patted
the deck beside him in invitation. Briefly, she considered her tactics. To remain standing and aloof was
no doubt the wisest course, but she would hardly be
able to question him with her teeth chattering. So she
huddled down on the warm boards, keeping as much
distance from him as she could in the small patch of
clear deck.

In planning to confront him, she had forgotten how

unsettling was his smile. She looked away, mastering the temptation to gaze at him, and attempted to frame a question so penetrating that he would instantly confess his identity and his plot. In this she was hampered by the impropriety of addressing him by the only name she knew.

"Mr. . . . ?" she began.

"Drew," he countered.

"A name from your childhood?" she asked, recalling the friendly familiarity of his exchange with the earl's groom.

He laughed. "You do not trap me so easily, Meg," he said.

"Croisset called you *my lord*," she accused, the more sharply perhaps because she had turned to him and found his laughing blue eyes likely to weaken her resolve. "Are you a lord?"

"No," he answered easily, apparently undismayed by her question.

"Then who did you pretend to be?" She sat up straight, adjusting her position slightly so that she might confront him directly and compromising with the chill wind so that she might not be lulled by his smile. "There must be another spy, a *lord* who intended to steal the earl's papers and sell them to the French." The idea was exciting. Her thief might not be as wicked as he seemed.

"Perhaps Croisset merely flatters all Englishmen with titles," he suggested, to Margaret's frustration neither confirming nor denying her suspicion.

"No," she said, "that's not it. You were . . . are impersonating someone. That is why you changed your hair and clothes and voice before you met with Croisset. But why?"

He pulled Croisset's purse from an inner pocket and hefted it lightly in his palm, suggesting its weight. Money of course, she thought, and her spirits sank at the evidence of his greed. He had wanted more than Croisset offered; he had taken Croisset's purse; and he meant to be paid yet again by the Viper.

"But surely," she said, reasoning aloud, "the sapphires you gave me are worth as much as any papers the French might buy." The glances of the rude sailors had cautioned her to tuck these away in a pocket of her cloak.

"Then you see why I must replenish my coffers," he replied.

"I don't see at all," she answered. "You could take back the sapphires and be rich, and then you would not need to sell any papers to the French. You and I could return to England, and I could slip the papers back into the earl's library with no one the wiser."

"Except Croisset, of course," he said dryly.

Of course. Margaret did not like to think of Croisset's rage when he woke and found them and his money gone. His vengeance would be terrible if he caught them, and she was sure he would try. And if the angry Frenchman did not kill her thief, surely English justice would. But, she reminded herself, if she could recover the papers or prevent their sale to the French, he would not be guilty of treason after all. It was no more than Prudence would do for Tom True.

"But you have fooled Croisset once and gained a fat purse. Might we not fool him again?"

"And what would be the gain?" he queried coolly.

"Your life," she answered, and blushed for the intensity with which she had said it, hurrying into further speech. "And the good of your country and the respect of all good men and women."

He laughed, but it was not the teasing laugh she found so pleasant. "At least one of those rewards might be worth something," he said, "but no gold?"

"I can hardly promise you gold," she retorted, affronted that he had shown greed in the face of her concern. She turned her head away so that he would not see her bitter disappointment.

"Alas," he said, "without gold, what will I do when I want to give some brave girl a bauble?" Margaret felt his fingers touch her chin and yielded to their gentle insistence that she turn back to him. He was kneeling beside her on the deck. "And if I give up my wicked ways, will I win your respect?" he asked quietly. Untrusting, she studied the handsome face so close to hers. She could detect no deceit in its clean lines and fair features. But if she offered her respect, something of herself, would he really abandon his treason?

"Yes," she said, "if you will turn the papers over to me and allow me to restore them to the Earl of Haddon, I will respect you." In her eagerness to persuade him she swayed forward slightly.

"I can't," he said.

"Oh," she cried, in the grip of an emotion quite new to her. He had played upon her hopes. The brightness of his eyes had deceived her again. While she took it for the fire of purpose, it was merely the gleam of greed. She pulled at her skirts and cape so that she might rise and flee, but he caught her by the shoulders with his strong hands and subdued her resistance by the simple expedient of wrapping his arms about her in a tight embrace.

"Meg," he began, speaking down at her averted face, "I said *I can't*, not *I don't wish to*. I do what I must do, and when I have done it, I shall restore you to your family. Now," he continued, "I shall go below so you may stay here to enjoy the sun and breeze, but it would be well if you were willing to negotiate a truce with me." He released her, and she felt his gaze on her as he waited for her reply. She held herself rigidly still and refused to look at him until she could command her voice properly.

"I may be forced to accompany you," she said, "but I do not choose to be on familiar terms with a thief and a traitor." He was gone almost as soon as the words were spoken, and if, after he left, she found her cape inadequate protection from the chill breeze and occasional spray, she would not admit it, even to herself. When the sun set on her second day at sea, she numbly made her way back to the cabin.

On her return, changes in her cabin were immediately evident. Someone had straightened the berth and brought fresh water and made other arrangements for her comfort. Across the blanket lay a man's cambric nightshirt. When she lifted the article and examined it she found it had been peculiarly altered, the sleeves chopped short and a hasty seam taken up the back in regular though unsightly stitches. It was too small a garment for any man she had seen aboard the ship, so it must be intended for her, strange as that seemed. She hung her cape upon its hook and saw once again her rumpled muslin. What a pleasure it would be to doff her limp, soiled dress. She had reviled her captor, and he had provided for her comfort. Her last thought that day was that she did not hate him as she should.

The third morning of her voyage new sounds and rougher motion woke her. It was rain she heard, passing in driving gusts across the roof of the cabin. Where was he, she thought, and immediately reproached herself for not wondering instead how her parents were taking her disappearance. Yet the otherness of her circumstances, the unfamiliarity of everything around her, made her parents seem impossibly remote. She had a vision of them making calls, entertaining guests, sitting in their drawing room, her mother at the pianoforte, her father with a book, as if she had never existed at all.

For the first time in her odd journey, the hours seemed to drag. She huddled in the berth or paced, while new thoughts distressed her about what would happen when they reached their destination. If she were to recover the stolen papers and escape her captor somewhere in Portugal, how would she find someone trustworthy and willing to undertake the trouble and expense of restoring her to her parents?

In the unsettling darkness of the storm she could not tell the time and believed the day would never end. When at last a leering sailor brought her evening meal, she found that even the wine could not make her sleepy. She squirmed and stretched upon her bed and thought the same thoughts repeatedly. Only when the storm subsided a bit and the boat resumed its steady rocking did she fall into a restless, dream-disturbed sleep.

She dreamt a swirling scene of confusion in a great London ballroom where she must perform all the steps in the sets with no partner until at last a partner seemed to come for her. Her mother smiled at her from among the chaperones, but as the other gentlemen made way for her partner, she saw that it was Croisset, and she turned and ran out into the garden. Yet there was no garden, only a noisy street where the mob pushed and shoved so that her feet could not touch the pavement and she was carried forward against her will. The surging crowd stopped at last, and she looked up to see a gallows, and with the strange prescience of a dreamer she knew for whom it stood. Two officers of the law roughly pulled forward her thief. In waistcoat and breeches, he looked as he had in Humphrey's stable, save that his arms were bound behind him. His eyes seemed to meet hers at once. When they lowered the rope around his throat, Margaret's own cry woke her.

She sat up in the dark, gasping, her heart pounding, and willed away the horror of it.

"Meg," came his voice, wondrously near, from the floor, she thought. "You were dreaming. You are quite safe for the moment." She could not get her breath to answer at once. "If not *quite* safe, at least somewhat safe," he continued. "The captain assures me his boat has made the crossing in far rougher weather."

"You, here?" she managed to say.

"Have our adventures frightened you?" he asked.

"No, it was something else entirely," she replied. She could not tell him she had cried out in fear for his life.

"Croisset did not frighten you?"

"Croisset? Yes, but truly, I . . . I was dreaming about the season," she said. There was some truth in that.

"You cried out in fear of Lord Leadfeet and Lady Loosetongue? I cannot believe it." From the gloom below she heard his low laugh.

"It was my first season," she said, wondering at herself that she could once again enter into conversation with him so easily. Nevertheless, she rolled onto her side and propped herself on one elbow to talk to him. In the blackness she could see nothing, not even an outline.

"Of course," he answered, "had you made your come-out a year ago, I would have . . ." There was a pause in which she found herself listening most intently.

"Would have?" she prompted.

"Would have found you less honest now," he concluded.

"Me, less honest? When you . . ." She could not finish.

"Do you wish to call me names again, Meg? Did I tell more lies in Dorset than you did in London?" The bitter tone of this remark made her wish she could see his face, and yet she was grateful he could not see hers.

"I did *not* lie," she protested.

"Ah, then you cannot have had a very successful season."

"It's true."

"Forgive me," he said, "I had no cause to abuse

you with such a comment. You must have attracted your share of admirers?"

"Not one. I was quite unnoticed, I assure you. My mother . . ." She fell silent, remembering her parents' disappointment in her. Her companion did not press her. After a time she asked, "Who are you?"

"You know my name, Meg."

Again she wished she could see his face. "I know the name your friend called you."

"And you will not use it. You prefer *thief* and *traitor*?" His voice was cold.

At the harsh words, she blushed in the darkness. She remembered the flash of something in his eyes each time she had reviled him. He was those things; he deserved her contempt and the contempt of all loyal Englishmen, and yet she wished to go on talking to him in the close darkness, did not dislike him as she should.

"I shall not revile you again," she promised, but she did not say she would use his name. "Croisset believes you to be a London dandy, a peer; that is who you pretend to be among these men."

"You think I am something else?" He sounded amused now.

"Yes, but did you not say that we see what we expect? Perhaps I am deceived as well," she admitted.

"If you have learned that lesson, then I am afraid I shall not be able to deceive you long, Meg." He laughed. "Best sleep now; we reach Portugal tomorrow."

"You mean to sleep here, with me?"

"With you?" he asked. "Is that an invitation?"

"No," she said at once. Although his voice had been teasing, she clutched the blanket around her.

"Then I must continue to make a bed of this floor, for I have no other place, and our companions believe me to have very good reason to sleep in this cabin."

She knew he was grinning. All the puzzling cir-

cumstances of her nights and mornings were suddenly explained—his coat, her shoes.

"One last word," she pleaded. "If you wish me to
call you by name, you must tell me your family
name."

There was silence for such a long moment that she
doubted he was there at all. "I have no name," he
said at last. "I am no man's son."

"Forgive me," she whispered, understanding not
at all, knowing only that she had touched upon some
profound sorrow.

"Go to sleep, Meg," was all he said.

On the floor of the cabin the young man who called
himself Drew lay still until he heard the girl's even
breathing. Though he had slept little in three nights,
he found it impossible to do so now. For some time
he told himself that it was the discomforts of his cold,
rocking bed that kept him awake; but when he had
lodged one shoulder against the base of the berth and
one booted foot against the chest, he acknowledged
that he had suffered worse discomforts. The truth was
that the novelty of sleeping so near a young woman
whose beauty and courage he admired and yet not
sleeping *with* her was a bit unsettling. He had cause
now to regret all the touches of that first evening.

He had avoided her for most of three days. She
had much to complain of in his treatment of her, and
the worst of it was he meant to expose her to greater
dangers yet. He had entered the library with a reckless
disdain for what might become of him and a fierce
desire to check his enemy, and she had stopped him
cold with her honesty. Her gaze, clear and uncom-
promising, had been like no other woman's gaze.
There had been nothing of seduction and everything
of herself. And he had seized her. He had not considered his motives in the event; he had been, as he
always was, caught up in the exhilaration of the game.

Well, he had played desperately and won. Until she had called him traitor he had not realized that he had also lost.

He had compromised a young woman of noble birth and remarkable character to whom he could offer nothing—not position, not fortune, not name. To protect her in the weeks ahead, he must claim her as his mistress, yet he meant in time to return her to her parents, heart-whole, as innocent as she now was. And somehow he would preserve her reputation as well as her life.

Once, on a dare, he had climbed into the ring at Grantham with one hand tied to his side, and faced the local champion. He had won the match to the cheers of all his friends, but his ribs had ached for weeks. On that thought his eyes at last closed.

Margaret's first conscious act was to prop herself up so that she might see the floor. Had she dreamed her encounter with him? To her surprise he had not wakened before her but lay wedged between her berth and the opposite wall in what could hardly be a comfortable position. No light from the windows above had yet reached his face to rouse him. With his eyes closed, his hair tousled, and his limbs sprawled, he looked less the man and more the boy. But there were shadows under the eyes and a darkening of beard on his chin that dimmed the luster and vibrancy of him. His energies were not inexhaustible after all, she thought. His chest rose and fell with the steady rhythm of his breathing, and she recognized the opportunity she had wished for. She slipped from the bed, gathering the nightshirt about her, and stepped lightly over him so that she might reach the bottle-green coat upon its hook. The papers were not in any of its pockets. There was only a small pistol which she had not realized he carried. While it might be useful to him, she had never fired a gun and did not know the first thing about guns. She stepped back over him and knelt on his left in a tiny patch of floor. His head was awkwardly pillowed on his greatcoat, but she doubted the papers were there. No, the papers could only be on his person somewhere.

She examined the folds and creases of his waistcoat for any hint of the packet. She could detect nothing. The taut lines of the breeches about his hips and thighs could only be the contours of his body, from which she looked away. Still he had not stirred. Did she dare to unbutton the waistcoat itself, to feel along the ribs? It was unthinkable that she would touch him so. Though he had touched her often that first night, his touches, distracting as they had been, had always furthered his plan. Well, she must accomplish her own plans. She must stop him from betraying England and save him from the gallows of her nightmare or worse.

She sat back on her heels and clenched and unclenched her hands, nerving herself for action. As lightly as she could she slipped the first button free of the restraining silk. She glanced at him; his eyes remained closed. Again she reached for one of the tiny buttons. She had unfastened five when she paused in her labors. She had opened a distinct gap over his heart; but so many buttons remained, and her progress was so slow. She could not expect him to remain asleep much longer. In desperation she leaned over him, the fingers of her left hand spread and pointing toward his waist. Lightly she rested her palm against his chest, allowing her fingers to feel delicately for the upper edge of the packet.

"Good morning, Meg," he said. He did not move. "Do you care to explain yourself? Or may I place whatever interpretation I like upon the present circumstances?"

She withdrew her hand at once, her face burning, feeling oddly conscious of her body under the loose-fitting nightshirt. "I hoped to find the earl's papers," she admitted.

"You searched the green coat?"

"I did," she replied, unable to look at him.

"I trust you left me my pistol, in case we should need it."

"Yes."

"Well then, you must satisfy yourself that the stolen papers are not on my person."

At that she looked up. "Oh, no, I could not," she said, shaking her head emphatically.

"But I insist," he replied. "It will be good practice for the role you must play in Portugal."

"Role?" she questioned.

"You are safe in this company, Meg, only as long as our companions believe, as Croisset did, that you are my mistress."

"But I could never be your . . . I could never touch . . ." Why did she hesitate? Why did the words seem like lies?

"Not *be*," he said quietly, "*play*."

"But I do not know the least thing about mistresses or what they must do or say, and surely I do not look . . . look . . ." She faltered.

"In that garment, I assure you do look . . . quite."

She was watching his face now, and only his evident amusement at her expense enabled her to regain a bit of composure.

"Very well." She leaned over him again and pulled at the remaining buttons determinedly, but her haste made her clumsy so that she lost her balance and would have fallen on him except that he caught her by the shoulders. To her great discomfort he held her there, her face just inches from his, his heart beating against her hand, his eyes, blue as deep water, urging her closer. Abruptly he pushed her back onto her knees and rolled away from her. He rose and turned from her to gaze out the window above the water stand, his fingers deftly fastening the buttons she had released. She retreated to the berth and pulled the blankets about her. She thought she heard him say something. "Fool" it sounded like, but the word was too faint for her to be certain.

Without turning he spoke again. "Do not be alarmed, Miss Somerley; I shall not require another such show of desire from you. You have only to dress the mistress' part and allow me to do the lying." More quietly he added, "I believe our lives depend on it. Can you do it?"

"Yes," she said. In the same quiet voice he explained what he had gleaned from the captain and crew about the men the Viper would send to meet them and how Croisset managed with such escort to convey messages beyond the English lines. In parting he urged that she wear the sapphires.

"If anything should happen to me," he said, "the jewels will buy you protection and a safe passage home."

"I could never sell them," she protested. "They must be returned to their rightful owner."

"The woman who owned them is dead, Meg." He paused. "Until this afternoon, then." He bowed and turned.

"Wait," she cried, as a new thought occurred. "What am I to call you before others?"

"My lord, of course." She was relieved to see him grin again and offered him a smile of her own.

5

FROM THE SOUTH railing Margaret watched the shore where cream-colored buildings with red-tiled roofs climbed steep hillsides. She had taken her position hours before when the land was no more than a blue outline above the eastern horizon, and had watched through all the transformations their approach had wrought, through an hour in which everything before her had been rosy in the setting sun's light, the windows flashing gold, then through still another until she could see browns and greens and the cream of the buildings and at last people on the beach. All hands were now on deck, each with some task necessary to maneuver their craft through dozens of others of every description. Margaret knew Drew would join her at any moment. Imperceptibly she had accepted the name in her own mind though she refused to speak it.

Since morning she had berated herself repeatedly for misusing an opportunity to stop him and for being so foolish as to smile at him. Eager to escape the scene of her weakness, she had dressed with haste and left the cabin. Now she meant to be strong-minded, to remember at every moment that he was a thief and a traitor, to keep her reserve and to be awake to any chance to recover the earl's papers. She must not allow him to leave the port with them.

"Meg," he said at her side, catching her by surprise in spite of her determination to be on guard. "Do you like this view of Oporto?" She turned to him, but did not answer. He was once more the dandy he had been for their meeting with Croisset, his greatcoat giving him an impressive breadth of shoulder. He had shaved, so that his face was boyishly smooth and fine. She looked away at once, repeating to herself the words that ought to condemn him. *Thief, traitor.* As if he sensed her reserve, he began to speak inconsequentially about their surroundings, pointing out ships and rigging, birds wheeling overhead and black-shawled women hunched on the beach.

"You have been here before?" she couldn't help asking.

"Some years ago," he replied in the guarded way he had when she asked for something of the truth from him.

Their vessel now passed between other larger ships in a long row and, at an opening among these, turned into the wind. With a sudden flutter the great sail went slack and came down, and the sailors scrambled to tie it to the boom, to drop the anchor and tie a line to another vessel. The captain accepted more of Croisset's gold, ordered the dinghy lowered, and led his men over the side.

When they were alone, Drew took Margaret's chin in his hand, turning her face to his. "Our escort will come for us now. Remember, you are Meg Summers, my mistress." His eyes, deep blue in the twilight, were cold with command, with the haughty air he adopted with the dandy clothes. "Your life depends on it."

"Of course, my lord," she answered, meeting his gaze squarely.

* * *

In minutes they heard the splash of oars. Though it was now dusk, Margaret could see a curious contrast between the two men in the approaching boat. The first was a large man with a robust massiveness, like a sturdy oak, and a shaggy head of reddish brown hair and a beard to match. He pulled the oars as if they were mere sticks instead of great beams. He pulled himself up the rope ladder in a single swift movement and stood frowning down at them. As he spoke in the odd French Margaret had first heard the sailors use, the other man came up over the side of the boat. He was not small except in comparison to his companion, but as sleek as the other was shaggy, dark-skinned and dark-haired, not quite handsome, his eyes too quick-moving and his lower lip pushed against the upper in a way that suggested displeasure.

After very little talk, both men turned to her, and Margaret guessed that Drew was explaining her presence. She kept her head proudly lifted, her gaze steady. The shaggy man gave her a leer, the sleek one, a coldly assessing look. Then the two men turned to each other, the sleek one speaking rapidly and gesturing for emphasis, the shaggy one responding in grunts and nods. As strange as their language was to her, Margaret recognized their exchange as a dispute. A terrible knot of fear pressed against her chest so that she could not draw a deep breath. She did not like to imagine the danger she and Drew would be in if these two men knew the turn they had served Croisset. Drew slipped an arm about her waist and pulled her against him. Speaking with the same arrogant impatience with which he had addressed Croisset, he drew forth the purse that had so far smoothed their way.

"My lord," she murmured into his chest, "are we to go ashore?"

The gold seemed to resolve the larger man, who stepped back, indicating that Drew and Margaret should pass to the ladder over the side. The smaller man said nothing.

Propelled by the large man's mighty strokes, their dinghy soon reached the shore and shot far up on a strip of sand. There Margaret was handed down to dry land and for a moment stood uncertainly, still rocked by the sea's motion. An open cart stood waiting, its driver apparently uninterested in the odd manner of their arrival or their lack of baggage. Above them the city faded into gray-blue indistinctness as they clattered through the twilight. Their way led continuously uphill, until Margaret felt the strain on the horse and knew they must stop. The last bit, the large shaggy man explained, they must travel on foot. They dismounted, and the two men closed around them, like guards leading prisoners, Margaret thought. They passed worn buildings stained with soot and rust, but covered with blue tiles like nothing Margaret had ever seen, so that she could not help but gaze in wonder. Hundreds of tiles composed pictures of heroes and saints.

The inn which they soon entered had but a few sailorish patrons in the taproom. The atmosphere was one of indifference, of letting one's fellow man go to the devil in his own way. A man lay sprawled across a table, apparently unconscious, while two others shouted violently at each other without arousing anyone's notice. Where was Margaret to find someone to confide in, someone to help her? The proprietess, a thin, shrill woman, smiled warmly at her companion, but dropped Margaret the briefest of curtsies and led them without delay to an upper room. It was an unexpectedly large apartment with a massive bed at one end, a bright fire in the hearth at the other and windows looking down the street and across the city. Drew gave the woman a few peremptory commands and the inevitable gold coin, and she hurried off. They were alone.

It was a circumstance Margaret felt she ought to welcome both as a respite from the looks to which her companion's lies had subjected her and as a chance to recover the earl's papers, but she was wary now of being alone with her thief. The very nearness of him seemed to weaken her best weapons—reason and conscience.

"Come to the window, Meg," he invited. Reluctantly she joined him, keeping her distance, and they stood looking out together.

"She's hardly a lady, this city, but she's not without her airs, her bits of lace or ribbon."

Margaret followed his gaze and saw the violet skyline like a lace border, the street a giddy distance below.

"You played your part well," he complimented.

Before Margaret could answer, the proprietess returned with a gleaming copper tub and a pile of towels. The shaggy man followed, bearing two great steaming cauldrons. At Drew's direction, they placed the tub before the fire and poured the bath.

"Your bath, Meg," he said to her as soon as the others had left.

Margaret stared at him, horrified, but he only laughed.

"I am going out and mean to be gone some time. Make use of my absence as you like." He gave her cheek a careless brush with the backs of his fingers. Then he was gone.

When his quick footfalls could no longer be heard upon the stairs, Margaret opened the door and stepped into the hall. The shaggy man was sitting in the dark at the head of the stairs, eating. He held a large bowl under his chin and shoveled heaping spoonfuls of its contents into his mouth. His beard glistened here and there where drops had spilled on it. At Margaret's appearance he put aside the bowl and patted his great thighs, gesturing that she should come to him. His gaze, rude and particular, took in her whole person and came to rest on her breasts. She retreated immediately, grateful that the door to this room at least could be locked. The shaggy man's laugh echoed after her. Of course she could not escape; her thief would never be so careless as to allow it. Resignedly she turned to the bath.

She had to acknowledge that the bath was most welcome and indeed it revived her spirits so that she waited with some impatience for Drew's return. He must have the papers on his person, and she must study him closely for some sign of the pocket in which they were kept. She could not fail in another awkward search of him. At his knock she unlocked the door and let him in. At once, however, her resolve to study him faltered, for his presence seemed to fill the room, and though she had backed to the window, she felt him too near.

"Come, Meg," he said, shutting the door behind him, "you must enjoy your adventure. See what I've brought you." He threw off his greatcoat and began emptying his pockets on the bed. There were combs and brushes and tooth powder, a man's shaving implements, and a serviceable black wool gown. "And most important," he said, reaching into his pocket again, "your book." He offered her a small leather-bound volume.

"A book?" she asked, drawing closer in spite of herself to see what it was. It was hard not to smile at him.

"It is not Horace, but surely your taste allows our English poets a place," he teased.

She was still staring, puzzled at his gift, when a single perfunctory rap sounded upon the door. The shaggy man entered and carried off the copper tub, sloshing its now-cold contents on the floor, the landlady scolding after him, her voice shrill in the hall.

The sound had scarcely died away when the pair returned, the shaggy man again setting down the tub and filling it with a second bath. Already Drew had shrugged out of his jacket and was sitting in the room's only chair, tugging at his boots. The shaggy man leered at Margaret.

"You don't mean to bathe," protested Margaret upon the exit of the two servants.

"Oh, but I do," he replied. He took her by the shoulders and propelled her to the bed, compelling her to sit up against the pillows. "This was to be my adventure," he continued, "and because I have been so good as to share it with you, does not mean I must forgo all my comforts. Read, Meg."

"It would serve you right, if I did not," she said, nevertheless holding the book before her face. For some minutes she turned the pages idly, pretending not to be at all disconcerted. The trouble was, her ears betrayed her. She heard his boots drop one by one and the clink of his watch and fobs on the table, the rustle of his garments, and at last the slosh of the water against the copper sides of the tub. Her face burned more than it had the first night in the cottage, and she didn't see a word on the page before her. She rolled onto her stomach and propped the book against the pillows, recalling suddenly the Latin poems she had attempted to read while Drew had changed that night and the piles of books on the floor of Humphrey's cottage.

"Humphrey was your tutor, wasn't he?" she asked. His silence assured her that she had hit on a truth of his past. He had had a gentleman's education whatever his career had been.

"Read to me, Meg," he ordered, his voice startling her with its low intensity.

"What do you like?" she asked.

"The 'Rape' if it's there," he answered.

"'Of the Lock,' of course," she said, refusing to be

further embarrassed. She thumbed through the pages for Pope's masterpiece. " 'What dire offence from amorous causes springs,' " she read. " 'What mighty contests rise from trivial things ... Say what motive ... could compel a well-bred Lord t'assault a gentle Belle? O say what stranger cause, yet unexplored, could make a gentle Belle reject a Lord?' " At first the phrases served only to remind her of her awkward situation, but soon she lost herself in the fair Belinda's world where the myriad sylphs tried in vain to guard the precious lock. Her awareness of the naked man in her room faded, so that she was surprised when he next stood beside her, dressed.

They dined in a small, dark room on indistinguishable dishes with exotic names and strong sauces of onions, garlic, and tomatoes. It was an occasion for much laughter as he played the proud lord with their hostess and the tease with Margaret when they were alone. Her fork was at her lips when he inquired how she liked tripe. She could not be sure of anything after that, but the dish he identified as *bacalhau*, cod, was tasty and satisfying. She drank sparingly of the wine, knowing she must not dull her wits in his company. At the end of their meal was an orange, opened on its dish like an exotic flower, the sticky-sweet juice leaving its perfume on her fingers.

They laughed a great deal, mostly as he teased her about London or mimicked with dreadful accuracy the affectations of the *ton*. But from time to time she fell silent, wondering how she was to eat with him, talk to him, indeed sleep in the very same room with him and remember what a villain he was and what he meant to do and what she must prevent.

She had been laughing at his teasing as they ascended the stairs, but at their door her laughter died as she began to fear the awkwardness of their retiring together for the night. But he excused himself and returned only when she was in bed, the blankets tucked securely under her chin. Then he made such minor preparations for sleep himself as removing his boots and jacket and cravat and blowing out their last candle.

In the darkness she heard him lie down upon the floor. She lay perfectly still and advised herself to sleep, but sleep wouldn't come. He had been the adversary of her waking hours for four days, but only the night before had she discovered that he slept on the floor beside her. Knowing that he lay so close in the darkness unsettled her. It was hard to think of the earl's papers, and to think that she must slip from her bed and try again to search her thief as he slept made her feel hot and shaky. She turned restlessly in the wide bed. She ought to do something. She thought of Prudence in her blue dress on every white, waking page of her book, but what would Prudence say to Tom True alone in the dark?

"Meg," he asked, "is there something you need or wish?"

"No," she said.

"But you cannot sleep?"

"Can you?"

"Not if you cannot."

"I have never shared a room with . . . anyone," she confessed.

"Then you must not judge from this occasion," he replied. "Neither a husband nor a lover commonly takes the floor." The words spoken with just a hint of wryness made her yet more conscious of the empty expanse of the bed around her. Her thief was too near. His nearness weakened her, made it impossible to think reasonably. She must get him to move.

"You cannot be comfortable," she said firmly.

He did not reply at once, and when he did, she detected again the wryness in his words. "My comfort must necessarily mean your discomfort."

"Could you not have the landlady make up a second bed?" she asked, striving for a reasonable, practical tone.

"It must appear that only one bed has been slept in. Our landlady is as much in the Viper's pay as are our friends, Shaggy and Sleek."

"Then everyone around us is an enemy, yours as well as mine."

"Yes."

"So would we not be wise to flee now, this very night? Can the Viper have so much gold to offer that you will risk your life for it?"

"Yes."

"Why are the earl's papers so very valuable to the French?"

There was a moment of silence. "Because they will enable the French to anticipate Wellington's movements this spring."

"Suppose Wellington moves before the Viper can get the papers?"

"Then the papers would be worthless."

"Then I do not need to get them from you," she said, unable to keep a note of relief from her voice. "I need only to delay your journey."

"Ah, Meg, you are too honest. If you mean to thwart the enemy, you must not reveal your thoughts so readily to him."

A sudden lump in her throat made it difficult to speak. She had been telling herself he was the enemy to be condemned and reviled, but to hear him acknowledge as much was painful.

"I must lie to you, deceive you, become dishonest myself to do my duty," she said, knowing that she could not disguise the unhappiness in her voice. He was silent for a time, and when he did answer, his voice, though careless, had the bitter edge she sometimes heard in it.

"At least then you will be ready for your next London season," he said.

She refused to answer, but all the satisfaction she gained from her stubbornness was that she believed him still awake when at last the ache in her throat subsided and she closed her eyes.

She woke to find herself alone. There was little to do to complete her morning toilet except to arrange her hair and put on the black dress Drew had borrowed for her. There was a glass, however, and the comb and brush he had given her the night before, so she took some pains with her hair. The only sign of her companion was a faint scent of soap and spice that told her he had shaved as she slept. She picked up the stubby brush with its still-damp bristles and felt a sudden curiosity about him. What had he looked like with lather on his face? What had he looked like as he bathed the night before? It was an awkward, uncomfortable thought that made her grateful to be interrupted by a sharp rap on her door.

She opened it to the shaggy man, who indicated with gestures that she was to precede him down the stairs. They made their way to the small parlor in which she and Drew had dined the night before. There, with a map spread before them on the table, Drew and the sleek man sat talking. Drew rose at once to greet her and lead her to a chair by the fire. She saw that he was acting the dandy lord again. He commanded a small table and a plate of sweet rolls with tea be brought to her side, but he showed no inclination to include her in the discussion. For a time no one regarded her, so Margaret ate and listened, discerning some familiar words in spite of the accent. The phrase with which the sleek man addressed his shaggy partner was so common as to be unmistakable—*mon frère*, my brother. As she began to pay more attention to their talk, she thought he used it when he wished to change the other's mind.

The shaggy man said little but ate so steadily and

with such apparent indifference to what he put into
his mouth that Margaret would not have been surprised had he consumed the china. The sleek man,
like Drew, had pushed his plate away. His attention
was all for Drew, his gaze like a cat's on a bird, and
though he often smiled, she sensed his impatience.
She thought it odd that the two men should be brothers. They did not particularly look like brothers except
perhaps about the eyes.

When the shaggy man picked up a bowl and began
to spoon some sort of stew into his large mouth, Margaret suddenly recalled a character out of her childhood, out of her father's reading to her. He was Esau,
the man of appetite, the hairy man, the hunter; and
his brother was smooth-skinned Jacob, who tricked
Esau out of his birthright and their father Isaac's blessing. She wondered then which of this pair was truly
in command. They did not agree readily on any point
it seemed. The three men concluded their parley and
rose, the two brothers, at Drew's word, standing
aside as Drew offered Margaret his arm and led her
from the parlor. He did not speak until they reached
their room.

"I know your conscience is impatient and prompts
you to act against me today, but I ask you to wait for
my return." Margaret attempted to look away, but he
turned her face to his and held it there. "The papers
you seek are not in the room, and nothing is to be
gained for England or your conscience by exposing
yourself to the dangers of this city or our large friend.
Promise me you will remain here until I return."

"You told me I must lie to defeat you," she answered.

"Then lie to me when I return, Meg, but lock the
door when I go. The landlady will bring you a luncheon." She did not speak; she had been too compliant
from the beginning, and she did not wish to tie her
hands with a promise now.

Drew swore. He stepped forward, and always conscious of his nearness, Margaret retreated; but he caught her and took her in his arms. One hand pinned her wrists behind her waist and held her body pressed to his, the other held her head unmoving as his face descended toward hers.

"You can stop me, Meg," he said. "A word from you stops me, but I promise you nothing will stop our hairy friend if he thinks you mean to leave my protection." He paused, his eyes their coldest blue.

She wouldn't give in. He doesn't mean to do it, she thought. He means only to embarrass and confuse me as always. But he lowered his head still closer to hers. She could count his eyelashes, could smell the soap and spice of him. Still closer he bent, and she felt how odd it was to be pressed against him so that her heart beat against his ribs. When she felt his breath against her lips, she spoke.

"I swear," she said. He drew back then, but it was a moment before he released her. When he did, he turned from her, collected his greatcoat, and departed without another word.

It was quite dark when she heard his steps on the stairs and the shrill, scolding voice of the landlady. As soon as she unlocked the door, their eyes met; it was he who looked away first. He strode past her, followed by the brothers she now thought of as Jacob and Esau, Jacob carrying a pair of valises, and Esau carrying an armload of packages. The landlady came last with a tray of meats and bread and wine and a plate of oranges, opened as before, like flowers.

When Drew had dismissed the others, he threw off his greatcoat and poured two glasses of wine. Silently, he offered her one. She shook her head, and he turned from her, his wine in hand, to look out the window.

"You kept your word, though no doubt it has troubled your conscience all day."

"Yes," she said, acknowledging both truths.

"What must you do to ease that troublesome conscience of yours, Meg?"

"I must stop you, and if I cannot, I must hinder you in every way, delay you."

"You have, you know. Already we have delayed a precious day here in Oporto for supplies. Believe me, another horse was hard to come by. Your very presence will delay us further, for our party will travel more slowly on your account, and the Viper will hesitate to come out of hiding until he is quite sure of us. His hirelings are suspicious enough, I assure you."

"But," she said, "when the Viper does find us, you will sell the earl's papers to him."

He didn't answer, only drank more of his wine. Then he said: "To satisfy your conscience you must find them?" His gaze challenged her. "Well then, search me, Meg, I offer no resistance at all." He drained the glass of wine and turned toward her. She made no move in his direction. There was something careless and defiant in the grin he gave her that she did not trust. He shrugged out of his jacket and tossed it to her. "Search."

"You say that either because you have hidden the papers elsewhere, or because you think I am not bold enough to . . . to touch you," she objected, laying aside the jacket.

"Are you bold enough? After this morning you will understand if I think you reluctant at best." She looked away. "Have you thought what you will do with the earl's papers should you recover them?"

"No, except to put them in the hands of some . . . loyal Englishman." It was true she had not thought ahead.

"And if the Viper were to come upon us before you

succeeded in such a plan, do you know what we could expect from him?" She shuddered. "You guess, don't you, Meg? Slow death for me, and much worse for you."

"Still, there must be something I can do to . . . stop you." She hardly realized she had spoken the words aloud.

"Nothing," he said gently, "except what you are doing, delaying our journey, causing division and suspicion in our companions."

"Then I will continue. I will do all I can to delay you," she vowed.

"I expected nothing less," he said. "Your wine, Meg."

She could not be so cross as to refuse the glass he offered, and to refuse to eat would simply be foolish. It was a while, however, before she recovered something of the ease she had felt with him the night before.

Their conversation faltered when they came to the oranges, and then he said, "But Meg, you have not asked about my purchases." She did not resist when he took her hand, so changed was his tone. At his urging she opened the parcels on the bed and was astonished at all they contained. There was a day muslin in pale blue and an evening silk in a deep wine red, the colors and daring cuts of which would have scandalized her mother, a creamy shawl of Norwich silk which she pulled about her shoulders immediately, a rather serviceable hat with a broad brim and little elegance at which she raised an eyebrow, and boots and gloves, and shifts and petticoats, and a filmy garment Drew told her she was to sleep in. As she held up the latter, she suddenly felt all the impropriety of her position.

"But I cannot wear any of these," she protested, recalling the demure fashions her mother considered suitable for a lady.

"You must," he insisted. "You have nothing else, and your life depends on your appearing a fashionable impure, as much as mine depends on appearing a dandy."

"Is this the way of it, then?" She studied the fringe of the shawl. "Does a man make such purchases for his mistress?"

"Oh, yes." He laughed. "And a house and carriage and endless strings of jewels as well."

"You have had a mistress, then?" she asked, not looking at him, though she wished to see his face.

"Once," he said. "A mistress is a rich man's plaything, and I am not a rich man. Open your last package, Meg." The last proved to be a black riding habit with maroon frogging and braid. "Try it on," he urged.

"Oh, no, I could not," she said, but his gaze told her he would not be denied.

"Where is your book?" he asked. She pointed to a low chest by the bed. "Tonight, I shall read." He sat on the bed and pulled off his boots, then stretched out as she had the night before with the book propped against the pillows. She realized it had been several nights since he had slept in a bed and wondered that he so readily took the floor each night.

"Where were we?" he asked. At her reply, he said, "To the end then, Meg." He began to read. " 'But since, alas! frail beauty must decay, / Curled or uncurled, since Locks will turn to grey; / Since painted, or not painted all shall fade, / And she who scorns a man, must die a maid.' " Margaret glanced at him then, sure from his tone that he was quite aware of her, but he had not turned her way. " 'What then remains but well our power to use, / And keep good humour still whate'er we lose? And trust me, dear! good humour can prevail,/ When airs, and flights, and screams, and scolding fail. Beauties in vain their pretty eyes may roll; / Charms strike the sight, but merit wins the soul.'"

Margaret struggled into the close-fitting habit as he read. The skirt was smooth across her stomach, and the heavy fabric seemed to mold itself over her hips. It was a new sensation to wear such a gown after her loose muslins. She had not been so conscious of her form before and wondered what he would think and how he had chosen a garment that fit her so exactly. She interrupted him shyly to say she was ready. He closed the book and rolled slowly onto his back.

"Come here," he said. She shook her head. He swung his feet to the floor and stood, adopting a grave air and circling to inspect her, his scrutiny causing her to blush hotly. It was nothing like the times she had shown a new gown to her father.

"You make an admirable mistress, Meg," he said at last, just when she feared he meant to embarrass her further. "Best go to bed now, we leave Oporto early tomorrow." He took up his boots and jacket and stepped quietly from the room, leaving Meg oddly disappointed and lonely and eager to lose herself in sleep.

On the floor Drew stretched, then allowed his muscles to fall slack. He was weary, and he would need to be more clearheaded, more ready to act in the days to come than he had ever been in his life, but Meg's presence in the room disturbed his sleep. He heard the covers rustle when she moved and her light breathing when she lay still. Well, it had been a long time since he had lain with a woman and two years since Lydia had made a fool of him, and of his brother, of course. At first he had taken comfort or revenge in various beds, but he was not a man who could take a woman's love or her body and give nothing in return. When through his brother's revenge he had been banished from the *ton*, he had turned from

women. It had been easy to turn from the London
beauties, who would never be so foolish as to love
him for himself. It had been harder to turn from the
barmaids and farmers' daughters, who would have
given themselves freely and who would have lost the
most. But he had, so now, he told himself, his discomfort was only his body protesting the denial of its
desires.

Still, Meg was unlike any woman he had known.
Another woman would have feigned interest or desire
to get close enough to take the papers, or used her
own body as a lure to draw him close. But Meg had
no notion of the power she might have over him. He
meant to leave her innocent, but it was so tempting
to tease her, to watch her unguarded eyes reveal her
honest feelings. From the beginning her honesty attracted him. He wondered how long she would hold
on to the truth in this conflict with him. He would
be sorry, he realized, if she gave up and began to lie.
He could, of course, tell her who he was and what
he was attempting to do, but he could not offer her
marriage. As a baron's daughter, an heiress, she could
not marry him; and as long as she continued to think
him a thief and a traitor, she would not consider mar-
rying him even though he had compromised her. So
great was her contempt for his misdeeds that she had
yet to say his name.

Of course, her regarding him as a traitor also meant
she was likely to endanger herself in a foolish cause.
He had been furious this morning at the possibility
that she might expose herself to rape or worse at the
hands of the shaggy man. Indeed, he had told himself
that his use of force against her was justified to keep
her from harm, but now in the darkness beside her
he doubted his reasoning. Perhaps he had used force
against her because he had wanted, just for a moment, to hold her. She was not a great beauty. Aboard
ship in her bedraggled muslin, she had looked like

something of an urchin. In a London ballroom he might have overlooked her. Their gazes might never have met as they had in the library of Haddon. But when he held her, he felt her womanliness, and the widow's habit he had found for her confirmed what he had discovered that morning—her form was softly rounded and fuller than he thought. Still it was only the circumstances of the game, this pretense of theirs, that had reminded him in such a distracting way of the desires of the flesh. He was glad for the long days of riding and constant danger ahead. These nights in Oporto had been like a rest period agreed to by the players in a game; now he must summon his energies to play in earnest again.

6

I N THE DAYS that followed, Margaret found herself
more than a little embarrassed at the absurdity of
her resolve to delay them. It had dismayed Drew as
much as a child's threats might dismay a giant. For
from the moment they began, it was clear to her that
her thief never intended to hurry to his meeting with
the Viper.

The horses were placid beasts, unwilling to respond to a rider's urging except to avoid the spur
or the lash. Drew, who rode the wind-swift Phantom, must have known the quality of such animals
at a glance. The narrow roads rose and fell sharply
with the contours of the steep valley, and often their
party was obliged to stop for one of the great oxcarts,
enormous cargo piled high and wide, solid wooden
wheels shrieking.

Drew showed an exaggerated concern for Margaret's comfort that led to frequent stops. And Esau,
though ostensibly the leader of their party, was more
apt to delay them than Margaret was. Every morning
of their journey, it required a bucket of cold water
from Jacob to rouse his sleeping brother. Esau would
emerge bellowing, his hair and beard streaming with

sparkling rivulets, his eyes promising vengeance against his brother. At a bland word from Drew, however, the big man would merely grunt and shake his shaggy head, sending cold drops flying.

This dilatoriness on Drew's part puzzled Margaret, for he had revealed to her that the value of the papers he meant to sell the French lay in part in the timeliness of their getting into French hands. Perhaps he did not wish the French to have the papers after all. She decided to test her theory with some delays of her own.

Whenever a bend in the road allowed a long view of the river below, she would pause. Unlike the lazy streams of England, the Douro was swollen and rushing, in some lights brown and in others silver, eddying and swirling around great boulders along the shore. Above it on either side rose steep, terraced hills, like wonderful cakes with hundreds of layers, each narrow layer green with the shoots of new grain, or white and pink with blossoming trees or vines in their unmistakable pattern of interlocking branches. At each delay Drew only smiled and pointed in the distance to some white village, dazzling against the surrounding green, looking as if no war had ever touched these hills. They would ride on.

Once Margaret stopped to watch the oddest vessel she had ever seen. It was a long narrow boat with a single sail bellying out over a cargo of casks on the forward deck, but the strangest thing about it was that the steersman in the stern stood high up on a crude lattice structure, rapidly swinging a great, long steering oar that trailed far behind the craft itself.

"Now there's a swift mode of travel for you, Meg," said Drew at her side.

"What is it?" she asked, turning to him for the first time that day. In the morning light, pale under low clouds, he was again the golden youth he had been when the earl's lamp lit his features. She lowered her gaze from his.

"It is one of the *barcos rabelos*, boats with tails, that bring the port down to the aging sheds," he said. "They are shallow enough to shoot the rapids, and the long oar makes them easy to turn. Should you like to ride one?"

When she hesitated, he spoke again. "You cannot tell me that the mare you are riding pleases you or that you would not rather gallop."

At this bit of teasing she dared to raise her eyes again. His hair made her think of the fairy tale of the straw spun into gold.

"You knew about the horses all along," she said.

"It is not our party that must hasten to this meeting," he said. "The Viper, when he hears we are up the Douro, will move swiftly enough. In some village will be his henchman who will report that a man wants to buy green wine; only then will the Viper come out of his rocky fastness to find us."

"Why must he be so cautious?" she asked.

"Because the *guerillas* of Don Julian Sanchez and others also move in these hills. They have yet to let a French dispatch get through."

There was little comfort for Margaret in these words. Her thief did not have to hurry as she had supposed, and the *guerillas* posed a new danger, for what if these fierce fighters for their nation's independence from French rule should come upon them and suspect their purpose? Perhaps her only course lay in staying with the thief long enough to discover where the papers ended up. She said nothing of her fears, asking instead about green wine.

"It isn't green, of course," said Drew, laughing. "*Vinhos verdes* are lemon-colored or rosy; the 'green' means they are young wines." He gestured across the river at the tiered landscape. "The growing season is not long enough or hot enough at this end of the

Douro for port grapes, but some of these young wines are quite good, light and sparkling, almost like champagne, or a pretty girl."

"Veenyoosh verdish," she repeated, mimicking his pronunciation, then falling silent as the import of his last words struck her. She did not know where to look. It seemed he would always disconcert her, always have the upper hand. She meant to match wits with him, not lose her own in gawking at him.

"You have a good ear for language, Meg," he said. "How much have you understood in this last week?"

On this safe subject she could answer him. "I understand more each day."

"Good," he said, "though best perhaps if our companions do not realize how much you understand. The village where we will make our next inquiries about green wine lies not too far ahead. Tell me if you wish to stop at any time along the way."

He rode ahead then to confer with the brothers, leaving her to ponder the beauties of the landscape, the dangers of her adventure, and the contradictions of her companion's character.

They had not journeyed many days when Margaret came to a better understanding of herself. Daily she thought of her missed opportunities for escape. For each one a number of reasonable objections came to mind just as they had at each earlier step along the way, but however reasonable her objections, the point she must face was that her mind objected to leaving him. Drew's taking her had exactly answered her own wishes. She had not wanted to return to London, ever, and each step of this odd journey had removed her farther from any chance of such a return. It had been days since she had thought of any of her past humiliations or of her mother's hopes for her.

The truth was she wanted this adventure, an unladylike admission that both dismayed her and gave her a curious satisfaction. She wanted to match wits with her thief, had wanted to almost from the moment she had stopped him in the library at Haddon. It was as if he had challenged her to a game.

At her mount's sluggish pace they plodded up and down the undulating river road for hours each day, the breeze at their backs, the sun, behind them, occasionally obscured by rain clouds. They passed dozens of villages, drawing stares felt but not seen, as if the houses had eyes. The eyes of their guides were often on her, too, and the feeling of being watched was one she now recognized instantly.

Then late one morning, at a place where the river changed, becoming more turbulent and muddy, they reined in before a low building. Beneath its tile roof was an open area of tables on a dirt floor. A crowd of little boys surrounded them, apparently shouting their willingness to do anything that might earn a coin from the elegantly dressed strangers. Even the patrons of the tavern rose from their chairs, enlivened by curiosity. Surely none of these was connected with the Viper, she thought. There followed the conversation for which Drew had prepared her.

Esau began their inquiry, meeting at first skeptical stares. The man's temper flared at once, causing the villagers to fall silent. Then Drew spoke in English and Portuguese.

"*Boa tarde, senhores,*" he began. "We are looking for green wines, your *vinhos verdes*. Perhaps you can recommend a fine vineyard, *quinta*?" he queried.

A spokesman, a man wiping his hands on a far-from-white apron, bowed and nodded and began to question Drew. "What did you wish, your excellency?" Jacob translated. "Something light and fruity, *branco*? Or something full and well-balanced, *tinto*?"

"Something for lovely ladies, something that sparkles as they do," Drew replied, and when this remark was translated, it seemed to be a cue for grins and jokes all round, at one of which, the crowd shouted appreciatively, and Margaret found herself the center of all eyes. She felt her cheeks heat instantly and lowered her gaze.

"Even in England," Drew went on, "I have heard of Aveleda and Castel Garcia, but you must know where the best wines of the Douro are to be found."

There was a brief, noisy debate, incomprehensible to Margaret. Then once more the spokesman was allowed to speak for all. "Do not be deceived, your excellency," came the translation. "There are no wines better than those of Senhor Fregata. Southsiders may make claims for the wines of Lamega, but the angle of the sun is such that the wines of the north bank must be superior." Again there was a general cheer of assent.

They were escorted out of the village, the last little boy following them until the few houses along the river were out of sight around a curve in the road. Clouds still rushed by on the breeze overhead, but their way was now steep and slow, or the drone of bees made it seem so. They ascended through uncultivated land, woods, and rocks. Hiding places, Margaret thought, conscious now that they had entered the region where the mysterious Viper operated. Yet no one appeared along the road or behind any of the outcroppings of granite. Only clouds piled up overhead.

Late in the afternoon they reached a tree-lined, cobbled drive. Esau was sent ahead to inquire if they would be received, and when he reported that the *senhor* himself wished to welcome them, they passed along the shady drive to the Quinta Fregata, a gracious manor unlike any structure they had seen so far in the country. Servants met them and helped them to dismount, and then the *Senhor* stepped out from the deep shade of an overhanging roof. Senhor Fregata looked like any English gentleman at home in the country. Indeed, in height and figure he resembled Margaret's father, but his hair was darker and thicker, his face tanned and lined, his chin dented and his smile very wide. "*Boa tarde, boa tarde*," he said. "You are most welcome, most welcome, *senhor, senhora*." This effusion of delight made Margaret feel decidedly uncomfortable. It had not occurred to her that they would deceive ordinary people, people who looked like her father.

"*Boa tarde*," returned Drew, stepping forward and extending his hand for the one their host was offering. "It is most kind of you to offer your hospitality to strangers, *senhor*. We were beginning to fear we would be caught in a storm." He gestured at the threatening sky above them.

"Permit me to introduce myself and my bride," he continued. The word jolted Margaret. *Bride* . . . It was what her mother wanted her to be. It had been the aim of Margaret's London season, but in London the word had conjured up visions of dresses and dinners and gatherings of relatives. Hearing it now on her thief's lips, it meant being claimed by a man, this man; it meant the intimacy of traveling together and other intimacies that lay beyond the bounds of what was proper for her to think. She blushed more furiously than she had at any of Drew's earlier teasing.

"Andrew Summers, wine merchant, and my wife, Margaret," he said smoothly, as if well-practiced in the deception, and as he spoke, he drew Margaret forward to make her curtsy and accept her host's handshake. Reluctantly she offered the *senhor* her hand, fearful that he would feel its unnatural heat as her whole body seemed to blush, and glad for the riding gloves that concealed her ringless fingers. When she could, she shot a quick glance of reproach at Drew for his blatant lie. She found Jacob staring at her. She lifted her chin and attempted to return his calculating look with a cool gaze of her own.

They were still standing in front of the house when lightning flashed and the first thunder rolled over them, bringing a downpour. Servants scrambled to snatch the baggage or lead the horses off, while Margaret and Drew were ushered inside. Their host preceded them, chatting happily to Drew in English and shouting orders unrestrainedly in Portuguese. Maids came running with a rustle of skirts and soft murmurings. Margaret could hardly look about her. She could not believe that she was about to impose on this unsuspecting man.

From above them as they ascended a large central stair came the excited chattering of distinctly young voices. Senhor Fregata stopped mid-sentence, clapped his hands sharply, and barked some order. Margaret was so startled at the sudden change in his tone that she looked up to see who could have earned a rebuke from so apparently amiable a man. All that she saw, however, was a flash of white skirts through the dark railings. She could not help but turn to her host who was looking most shamefaced. Her own expression must have betrayed something of her curiosity and surprise, for he confessed, "My daughters."

Margaret was still wondering at his embarrassment over his children when they reached a room of comfortable proportions and cheerful furnishings. Senhor Fregata himself pointed out the room's features and inquired anxiously if it would suit them, as if, finding the room lacking in the elegance to which they were accustomed, they would prefer to depart in a thunderstorm rather than stay another minute under his roof. Margaret had to admire her thief for his ability to reassure the older man and to express how grateful they were for this hospitality. But she could not wait to take him to task for his latest dishonesty.

She stood at the window, tugging at her gloves and watching the rain wash over vineyards and forest until the last of the servants left the room. In the ensuing silence the rain whispered against the distant trees, drummed on the roof, clattered down some drainpipe, and splashed against the broad-leaved plants below. Behind her, the fire set when they entered popped loudly. She turned to find her companion leaning against the mantel, regarding her thoughtfully. They had shared many rooms now, but his claiming her as his bride awakened that consciousness of him that, strive as she might, Margaret could not entirely overcome.

"This is very bad of you," she began.

"I know," he said, but his gaze did not waver.

"It was wrong to steal the earl's papers and worse to attempt to sell them to the French, though you have not yet done so," she continued, cataloging his crimes but determined to be just. "And it was wrong to deceive Croisset and knock him out and steal his purse though he is perhaps a worse villain than you are, and . . ."

"And it was most wrong to abduct you," he added, straightening and facing her directly. His willingness to accept her rebuke made her forget momentarily what she meant to say next.

"I do not blame you for that." she managed, her self-knowledge making her look away from the blue eyes gazing so intently into hers. "For I . . . I should have resisted you more from the start. But surely it is not necessary to take this pretense of ours so far that we must impose on Senhor Fregata. After all, to signal the Viper you have only to give the appearance of looking for green wine."

"Do you wish to leave?" he asked. "It is certainly possible, even now, though, I confess, I do not wish to get a soaking nor do I wish to disappoint the *senhor*, who seems so pleased to have our company." She had thought that too, that their host seemed extraordinarily pleased to welcome them.

"But it is a violation of everything decent to accept the comforts due a guest under such false pretenses. Could we not stay in some village or town nearby as we have before?"

"Undoubtedly," he replied, "but I hardly think a baron's daughter would prefer such accommodations as are available in this region."

"I would rather put up with some discomfort than lie to good people."

"You are willing, however, to lie to bad people?"

"No," she protested, "I only meant that I have been cold and wet and hungry before." Her companion raised an eyebrow. "Or if not so very uncomfortable, I could learn to be so."

"I am glad to hear you say it because very likely you will be cold and wet and hungry before we are through with this game."

"Game? Is it a game to lie to the *senhor?*"

He winced at her scorn as if she had caused him pain. "If I do think of our adventure as a game, an exercise of wits against a clever opponent, there is little I can lose in your estimation, is there?"

Margaret looked at the floor. Did he care then for her good opinion? And wasn't the game what she herself had admitted she enjoyed? But she had not thought others could be hurt in it. To lie to Croisset and the brothers did not trouble her conscience as perhaps it should, but the *senhor* was so like her father. What would her parents think if they knew the disgraceful role she had to play while traveling with her thief?

"Did you have to say we were married?" she asked, looking up. "I do not even have a ring."

"So," he said, his expression quite unreadable, "it is the particular lie that bothers you." He came toward her then, removing the ring from his little finger, and took her left hand. Solemnly he slid the ring down her finger. But the sensation did not stop there. It traveled up her arm like the spark up a fuse in a fireworks display she had seen at Bath.

She looked at the heavy gold with the single bright stone and, withdrawing her hand from his, turned away. She did not wish him to see her burning cheeks.

"I know it is not what you would choose," he said to her back. "I know you will accuse me of sophistry, but when Senhor Fregata sees you as my wife, he sees more nearly the truth than he could any other way. He sees a respectable young woman who deserves to be treated as a lady; and whatever your circumstances, Meg, you are a lady, and you have done nothing to merit his disrespect."

"Yes, I have," she said, momentarily reckless in her distress. "I have chosen the company of a thief and a traitor over the difficulties of escape."

She meant the words as a self-reproach but saw in his bleak expression that he had taken her words as a further condemnation of himself. He was so still she thought for a moment that he had stopped breathing. Then he moved, settling himself with apparent casualness in a chair by the fire and stretching his legs out before him.

"I beg your pardon," she whispered. "I promised not to call you such names."

"Do not refine on it too much," he advised. He stared at his boots, saying nothing, while Margaret wondered how to restore him to his customary teasing ways.

"Meg," he said at last, "there will be less hypocrisy in playing my . . . wife tonight than you will meet with in a morning call in half the drawing rooms of London." He paused. "But rest assured, I shall not ask you to deceive any more unsuspecting hosts. For the remainder of our journey we will make our beds where we can."

"Thank you," she said, puzzled that this victory over him should leave her feeling so dispirited. "Truly, I would prefer to be cold or hungry than to . . . lie again," she finished.

At that he laughed. "I doubt we will be so very cold, and you cannot imagine that our large companion will ever allow our party to starve."

"You mean Esau, I suppose, but he is not very nice in his choice of foods. I suspect he will eat things that you and I might find most unpalatable."

"Esau?" he queried.

She blushed. "For Esau and Jacob," she explained. "I have been calling them that in my mind because they remind me of the biblical brothers—the one, dominated by his appetites, and the other, calculating. They are always on the edge of a quarrel." She was surprised at the end of this explanation to find him looking at her with every appearance of admiration.

"I know it is a bit of foolishness," she confessed.

"No, it isn't, Meg; it's quite perceptive." His praise was even more disconcerting than his teasing, and she meant to prove him wrong about her astuteness.

"But I can hardly claim to be perceptive about such things. You see I have no brothers or sisters myself. And though I do have cousins, I can only guess about such family relations from what I read, and perhaps stories are not so very reliable a guide. This Esau and Jacob quite puzzle me. They seem enemies as much as brothers."

"Nothing should puzzle you less," he said frankly, but his eyes did not meet hers. "Brothers always make the most bitter enemies." There could be no doubt from his tone that he spoke from experience, but Margaret could not question him, for there was a knock on the door and the quiet maids entered, bringing a tub and towels and kettles of hot water.

"Where is your book, Meg?" asked the thief.

7

S ENHOR FREGATA BEAMED at them as they entered
his drawing room.

"Good evening, good evening," he said. He had
changed into a satin coat and breeches so outmoded
that they reminded Margaret of adult gatherings to
which, as a child, she had been admitted only to make
her curtsy. He bowed to her and shook the thief's
hand heartily. There were compliments for Margaret's
wine-colored silk that made her blush to match the
gown.

"Sit, sit," the *senhor* urged, waving his arm at a
group of ornately carved chairs. With his forefinger
he drew a quick circle in the air, a signal at which
two footman and the butler stepped forward. These
offered wine to Margaret and Drew almost before they
could seat themselves.

"So," said the *senhor*, "welcome to the Quinta Fregata. Drink, drink." He raised his glass to them, and
the thief raised his in return, offering a Portuguese
phrase that brought an even broader smile to their
host's face.

When the *senhor* had seated himself and they had
all sipped their wine, he began again. "Green wine?"
he asked. "It is not what Englishmen want, I think."

87

"Perhaps not," Drew replied, "but English ladies need something besides ratafia and orgeat."

"True, true," the *senhor* agreed, "but our green wines do not travel well."

"We will find a way," Drew assured him. "Even the Romans shipped wine all over the Mediterranean."

"You will do this alone?" It was a question age was bound to ask of youth.

"I have friends who will help me," said Drew, naming one of the great port houses. "If I can provide them with a wine worthy of their efforts, they have agreed to ship it." Margaret marveled at the ease with which he spun out his fiction. She could almost believe him, and she was sure the *senhor* did.

"A worthy wine!" The *senhor* laughed and held up his glass in which the pale liquid gleamed like gold. "How did you come to hear of our wines, Mr. Summers? You have been to our country before perhaps?"

"Some years ago," came the reply. It was as much as he had admitted to Margaret earlier, and she listened carefully for that note of reserve in his voice that always meant he was telling the truth.

"But you were not then looking for wine?" the *senhor* queried.

"No," said Drew, refusing to meet Margaret's eye though she gazed at him steadily.

"Perhaps you came as a soldier?" the *senhor* continued, seeming unaware of his guest's reticence.

"Yes," was all the reply.

"I guessed it, I guessed it. Were you with Moore?"

"No, I came with Wellington's forces when the command passed to him. He was mere Sir Arthur then."

"Then you were at Oporto," concluded the *senhor*, slapping his thigh.

"Yes, I was," agreed Drew, suddenly grinning at the other man, apparently unable to resist the *senhor's* interest. "Soult thought your river was all the guard he needed."

"But you crossed it, and a Portuguese led the way, a Portuguese," he insisted. "Ah, what a day, what a day for us."

"It was that. You should have seen the luncheon Soult meant to eat." Drew began to list the elaborate dishes left by the fleeing French and calmly eaten by the great Wellington himself.

"Well, well, we shall hope to serve you as well this evening. Come, come, we dine."

Once again Senhor Fregata gestured, and his footmen with perfect symmetry of motion reached to pull open the double doors of the drawing room. As they did so, there came a frightened squeal, and the doors swung in to reveal three little girls with identical dark curls and eyes, identical white dresses, and identical expressions of fear. They were holding hands so that they resembled a string of paper dolls such as Margaret's mother had made for her as a child. The youngest had fallen, and thus there was no possibility of escape for the eavesdroppers. The *senhor* looked wrathful, but before he could speak, Drew knelt and lifted the littlest to her feet. Then he bowed to them, saying good evening in their own tongue.

The *senhor* seemed to recover from his surprise so that when the three pairs of great dark eyes turned to him again, their expression pleading, he relented.

"Mrs. Summers, Mr. Summers, these are my daughters, Gabriella, Elena, and Ines." Each girl dipped a curtsy and rushed to hug the *senhor*. Again Margaret wondered at the odd mixture of pride and embarrassment in him as he presented his children. Her next thought was like a pang. How easy for a young child to please a parent. Before her London season she had hugged her own father just so a thousand times and received his answering embrace. The *senhor* spoke, apparently promising his reluctant children some treat, for they relinquished their hold on him and went off happily. Margaret found Drew observing her closely and looked away. She gave a little start to see Jacob watching as well from the shadows under the stair.

At dinner their host was as lively and full of talk as he had been from the moment of their arrival, so that Margaret and the thief were called upon to do more than their share of eating. And there seemed no end to the delicacies the *senhor* meant to press upon them. The momentary fear that had assailed her when she discovered Jacob watching them faded from her mind as the *senhor* questioned her companion about the details of campaigns and battles. Her thief could not be lying about such things, her heart told her, but her mind mocked her with a recollection of his own words, Men see what they think to see. Could he have been part of Wellington's army and now be willing to betray a man he had served, men who had been his comrades? She could not believe it, but if he were not a thief and a traitor, why was he trying to sell the earl's papers to the French?

A sudden silence between her two companions brought Margaret's thoughts back to the conversation.

"I never hear of the action now," the *senhor* was saying. "My son refuses to come home." For a moment he seemed to dwell on some inner sorrow; then once again he was gay and voluble, urging them up from the table and into the drawing room.

The tea tray arrived, but the senhor's preoccupation continued. He broke off his remarks mid-sentence and looked repeatedly at the double doors.

"Will your daughters join us?" asked Margaret, recalling the evenings in her childhood when her father had read to her and suspecting that the *senhor* very much wished to be with his children.

"Do not keep them out on our account, please,"

said Drew, taking a seat beside Margaret on a low couch. Senhor Fregata looked from one to the other of his guests.

"We have so few visitors, you see," he explained. "And my son comes not at all, not at all." He hesitated like a man about to plunge into cold water. "They are my *natural* daughters, you see," he said at last. He seemed to fear that Margaret and Drew would take offense at this revelation of the illegitimacy of his children and depart immediately, but he allowed himself to be persuaded by his guests, and the little girls were sent for. The servant dispatched, Senhor Fregata became cheerful again and eager to tell them his story.

"My son refuses to come home while they are here, but I will not cast them off," he told Margaret and Drew. "There is little enough I can do for them now. Oh, they will have tutors and finery and great dowries, great dowries, but not all the wealth of this *quinta* will get them the respectable matches they deserve." He opened his arms in an expansive gesture, then dropped them. "When I became a widower, I meant to marry their mother, but my son would not hear of it. While I thought I might persuade him, I delayed. Now it is too late." Again he seemed to be lost in contemplation of some inner vision. "Ines is dead." The *senhor* laughed bitterly. "Ines is dead. It is what you English call irony," he concluded, "a joke, is it not?"

Margaret looked to Drew, puzzled by the *senhor's* words. Was Ines the mother of the *senhor's* children? What did he mean it was a joke?

Drew took Margaret's hand, and intent as she was on what he might explain, she allowed him to hold it.

"It is a saying in Portugal that one uses when the opportunity for action has passed, when there is no longer any point in doing what one intended," explained Drew. "*It's too late; Ines is dead*. Senhor Fregata is telling us that the death of *his* Ines recalls the saying. There is a story behind the saying, is there not, *senhor*? A love story?'' Drew asked as Margaret withdrew her hand.

The arrival of the little girls with their nurse interrupted just then. Shyly each came forward to curtsy, encouraged by nods and smiles from their papa. Then he held out his arms to them, and the little girls scampered up onto his lap. There was an interval of squirming and arranging, accompanied by giggles, until all three children had managed to get as close as possible to their father. He whispered to them, and they became still, looking up with faces at once content and expectant. Margaret recognized the expression, the look of a child about to be told a story. She was sure she had looked at her father in just that way many times.

"Once, very long ago," the *senhor* began, pausing after each phrase to translate for his children, "there was a handsome, brave prince named Pedro for whom the king had arranged a marriage with a lady of Castile. Their marriage was to end the wars between Portugal and Castile. Pedro, who had not yet fallen in love with any woman, agreed to wed the lady his father had chosen. He journeyed to Castile, and they were wed in a great ceremony. His bride thought him handsome, and she liked being a princess with many attendants, but Pedro's heart remained untouched. Pedro returned to his own country to prepare a welcome for his bride, and she soon followed. As a princess, she brought with her from Castile many ladies-in-waiting. The loveliest among them was Ines Pires de Castro. Pedro fell instantly in love with her."

In his soft, rich voice, the *senhor* went on telling of the death of the princess, the secret marriage of Pedro and Ines, and ten happy years. Then the *senhor* described the return of the old trouble with Castile and the fear and suspicion of the court toward the woman who had such a hold over the prince. He told of the confusion and vacillation of the old king, the ruthless pressure of Ines' enemies, the heartless men who went in secret and slit Ines' throat.

At that Margaret gasped. Perhaps such things happened in novels, but her knowledge of history was vague on horrors. Once again, she allowed Drew to take her hand.

"When Pedro discovered what had happened in his absence, he was furious. His advisors counseled peace in vain. 'It is too late,' he said, 'Ines is dead.' He waged war against his father and won. He hunted down the men who had killed his wife and had their hearts torn from their bodies. Still his anger could not be satisfied. He had Ines' body taken from the grave and dressed as befit a queen, a crown on her skull. He locked all the nobles and their wives in the church at Coimbra and made them come forward one by one to kneel to his queen.

"His vengeance was nearly complete. He made all join in a procession of honor, accompanying Ines' coffin to the magnificent tomb he had prepared for her, all white and delicately carved. Then he waited to die. Oh, he did his duty, ruled his country, engaged in the pastimes of a prince, but meanwhile he prepared his own tomb, directly facing that of Ines. And he waits still, buried in his tomb, his feet at Ines' feet. He waits for Judgment Day, for on that day, when the dead awake, he and Ines shall sit up, and the first thing each shall see is the other's face."

The *senhor's* voice was soft as he ended the tale. His youngest daughter was asleep; the other two lay limply in his arms. He appeared much affected by the story, tears streaming down his cheeks past an incongrously happy smile. Drew squeezed Margaret's hand gently, and she stiffened at the reminder of the intimacy she had been allowing, enjoying.

"Mrs. Summers," he said softly but with wicked emphasis, "shall we help the *senhor?*" She caught his meaning at once. They rose and crossed to their host. Drew lifted the youngest girl and laid her gently on the couch he and Margaret had left. Margaret helped the older two to stand. When the *senhor* was free of his charming burden, he pulled forth his handkerchief to dab his eyes and gestured to his footmen.

The servants hurried about at his command while their host, somewhat recovered from the emotions that had overcome him, urged his guests to treat his house as if it were their own. Drew pleaded Margaret's weariness. A brief, muted debate followed. Then the nurse appeared. With quiet efficiency, she assisted the *senhor* in leading his sleepy children off to bed.

"Good night, good night," he whispered. "It has been a great pleasure, a great pleasure."

In the now-quiet drawing room Margaret felt how strong had been the influence of the *senhor's* story and the love it celebrated. It was a love like no love she had ever heard of outside of poetry. Yet the *senhor* told of it with the conviction of one who had lived such a love. It was not the gentle blend of affection and irritation that her parents lived by, and it was certainly not what they meant by the phrases with which they had described their expectations for Margaret's season. Ines and Pedro had hardly made "a proper alliance," or a "suitable connection." No, their sort of love was exhilarating, indifferent to society. She understood perfectly why the *senhor* had smiled through his tears and why she herself had been unmoved by the prospect of a proper marriage.

She and Drew were standing together, facing the door. Somehow, without intending to, she had fallen into the role he had assigned her, and it had been rather pleasant. With deliberate casualness she moved away from him.

"You expect me to be in perfect charity with you, I suppose," she said, adjusting her shawl, refusing to look at him.

"We did give a lonely man a great deal of pleasure with our . . . fiction," he replied.

"But he told us a truth he might have easily concealed, and we did not repay him in kind." It was less a true pang of conscience that prompted her to contradict him than a sense that she must resist him in any way she could.

"Yet there was a great deal of truth in our fiction, was there not?" he asked.

At that she did look at him. "What do you mean?" she asked. His question made her distinctly uncomfortable.

"I mean," he said, coming to stand directly in front of her so that it required some courage not to back away, "our interest in our host was genuine, our pleasure in the evening unfeigned. How often could you say that in London, Meg?"

She dropped her gaze from his heated one. Perhaps it was more dangerous to disagree with him than to agree. To cool their exchange she asked, "Do you think the *senhor* will keep his girls with him after all?"

"Yes," answered her thief, speaking in a milder tone and stepping back a little, as if he, too, wished to distance himself from her.

"But to do so means the *senhor* must often be lonely."

"He will be less so as they grow, and you cannot doubt his affection for them."

"No, but to keep his daughters must also mean that his son will be lost to him."

This time it was Drew who turned away. After a pause he said in a level voice, "Fathers have been known to cast off their sons." He continued, still without looking at her, "Shall we go up to bed then, Meg?" He offered his arm, and she took it uncertainly.

He meant to end all talk between them, and she guessed it was because she had touched a subject too near his own experience.

He led her to the foot of the stairs and stopped. "You go on ahead; I will follow shortly."

She nodded, a little disappointed by his words, but she did as he bid her, mounting the stairs slowly, conscious of his gaze upon her as she went.

As she reached the top of the stairs, Margaret wondered that the hall should be so dim. Surely it was not so late that the candles had burned down. The opening of a door at the far end of the hall made her turn. It was their own door, from which a shadow seemed to slip and glide along the wall. She stood perfectly still, but the fleeting figure disappearing into the darkness never looked back.

8

MARGARET TOOK A few cautious steps forward, her imagination darting ahead, examining the room itself and pursuing the shadowy figure. The room, she realized, could be examined at leisure, but the figure must be followed at once, if at all. It would not be one of the *senhor's* servants; they could have no motive for furtiveness. From the size and quickness of the figure she concluded it must be Jacob. What had he sought in their room—Croisset's purse? Or perhaps the papers? It had not occurred to her before, but if the brothers became impatient to meet the Viper, it was likely that they would try to steal the papers for themselves. Her racing thoughts impelled her feet forward so that she reached their door almost before she realized she was moving.

Once more she had cause to chide herself for her reluctance to act against Drew. If the papers were in the brother's hands, she would never prevent them from reaching the French. She had to know if Jacob had succeeded in finding them where she had so far failed.

Ahead of her the figure vanished in the gloom though no other door beyond theirs had opened. She glanced back but did not see Drew. For the first time since her abduction she was virtually unguarded. She hurried forward. When she reached the end of the hall, she understood the mysterious disappearance of the man, for she found herself at the top of a long stair with one turning. Dimly lit but serviceable, it led, she suspected, to the kitchens and storerooms below. She lifted her skirts with one hand and ran lightly down, sliding her other hand along the wall, her slippers and skirts rustling more faintly than pages turning in a book. Thus she caught the sound of a door opening and closing below her. At the landing she paused to look over the banister into the hall below. It was empty as she had expected, and there were several doors her quarry might have entered.

She descended a dozen more steps. The doors along the wall opposite the staircase were identical, dark and forbidding, but as she studied them, she saw that light came faintly from under only the second door. She considered going to the door itself, but a passing image of the *senhor's* daughters caught at their eavesdropping stopped her. She would have even less chance of escape. She chose to remain on the stairs, concealed from the door opposite by the banister. If she were lucky, the brothers would be together and they would quarrel. She knew she could hear Esau's voice from where she sat. If she were unlucky, Esau was somewhere else and would see her as he came to meet his brother. It would be impossible to escape him by running up the stairs.

These thoughts had occupied her for no more than a minute when she heard Esau's first loud exclamation. Muffled as the words were, she recognized the peculiar dialect that all those in the French employ seemed to use. Again he spoke, his voice louder still. This time she heard the word "*Ingleses*" and the words for "Viper" and "payment." She forced herself to concentrate. The next time he spoke, she caught every word.

"No. We can't kill him. Need him to signal the Viper."

She willed her heart not to pound so she would miss nothing, but the next words made little sense. Then Esau fairly burst with wrath.

"No. We let Viper kill him."

Dear Lord, did Drew know the danger they courted? No answer followed, and Margaret knew it was time for her to leave before she could be caught. She stood on shaking legs and felt herself seized from behind with a suddenness that momentarily deprived her of breath and pulse.

"Meg, my girl," came Drew's whisper at her ear, "you do have a way of putting yourself in danger." He turned her toward him, releasing her mouth, and she felt herself breathe again. "Come upstairs, love, and tell me about your adventure." The words were mild but seemed to come from between clenched teeth.

The room, when they entered it, appeared undisturbed. She attempted to pull away from him, but he did not release her. Instead he turned her to him and held her pressed against him as he had once before.

"How did you know where to find me?" she asked, drawing back as much as she could in his hold.

"You were not here; you had not come down the main stair; there was but one other possibility. I considered that you might be enterprising enough to climb out the window, but I did not think you would leave on such a night without your cloak. Why did you venture so near our untrustworthy guides?"

"I saw Jacob leave our room. At least I suspected it was Jacob, and I thought he might have taken the earl's papers."

"Because?"

"Because if they must reach the French soon, then he must be tempted to take them himself." Margaret had the satisfaction of making Drew look away.

"Suppose you had been discovered in your eavesdropping," he suggested, looking back at her.

"I meant to scream and fight. This is Senhor Fregata's house after all, and there must be servants about."

"As there were in the Earl of Haddon's house?"

This question caused her to look away. Her own part in her abduction, now that she understood herself, embarrassed her more than ever.

"I did not fight then, I know, but I would now," she assured him, daring to meet his gaze.

"Why didn't you fight me?" he asked in a different voice. It was not a question she wished to answer. She drew a deep breath.

"I . . . I preferred the unknown to the known." It was not precisely a lie.

"Were you so unhappy in London, Meg?"

"Yes, I was," she said.

"Why? Tell me," he said.

"Now? Like this?" she asked. The quality of his hold had changed in some indefinable way so that she knew he was no longer angry.

"This is to teach you," he said, giving her a slight shake. "You think you can defend yourself against a man. You blame yourself for your own abduction. You have not the least notion. Try to break my hold." He released her hands but held her waist.

To meet his challenge, to free herself, she would have to touch him, but her hands felt too heavy to lift. He was grinning at her, clearly aware of her dilemma. She thought of the proper ladylike responses to such liberties as he was taking—kicking a gentleman's shins, slapping his face. But she felt oddly warm and heavy, as if she might melt. His hands seemed to support her as much as constrain her. Then she recalled his advice to her once before. He was a man who could be stopped with a word.

"Why did you take me from Humphrey's cottage

that night?" she asked, looking boldly into his eyes.

As she expected, her direct request for the truth caused him to loosen his hold. She slipped free at once and stepped back. Even as he allowed her to distance herself from him, she saw he was considering his answer. He would not speak the truth impulsively as she always did.

"I took you," he said, "because I had to know the outcome of my meeting with Croisset before I allowed you to return and tell your tale. Humphrey was not expecting you, and had I left you bound and gagged in his cottage, I have no doubt his first act would have been to release you and yours to report to some authority."

So there *had* been an improvised element to his meeting with Croisset. Encouraged by this grain of truth, she pressed him for more. "Croisset would have killed you if he had seen through your disguise, but when he did not, you thought of taking his place as messenger yourself?"

He laughed. It was the only sign he gave that she had disconcerted him at all. "Meg, you are too clever by half, and I see I was wise not to leave you to report after me. Did you learn something tonight?"

"Oh, yes," she said, "that one of our brothers would willingly kill you and that the other would prefer to let the Viper do it." She reported exactly what she had overheard.

"Poor Meg, it is not what you are used to, but you are hardly frightened, are you?" he asked. He seemed to study her.

"Frightened enough," she replied. She did not wish to examine her fears too closely. "Do you still consider that it is a game we are playing, knowing that your companions mean to murder you?"

"They will not try tonight, however, Meg," he said. As he spoke he moved purposefully toward the door.

"Until he is sure of the location of the papers, Jacob will not kill me."

"He did not find them tonight, but are you so certain of tomorrow?" she asked. She was surprised at the sharp tone of her own voice and the sharp regret that he was again cutting off their talk.

"Hardly," he said, "but I do mean to carry on our journey. If we can outwit the clever Jacob for three days more, Holy Week will begin. Then every village will have its *romaria*, its festival. The Viper may move freely among the hundreds of pilgrims, and we may expect to meet him." The bland words had an unexpected finality to them.

"You mean to find him even though he intends to kill us?" She wanted to argue with him, to anger him again.

But his reply was mild. "I do. After all, the Viper has the gold." Once again he reminded her of his greedy purpose. He put his hand to the doorknob. "I will send a maid to you. Good night, Meg." Then he was gone.

When he returned, Margaret lay still in the big bed, feigning sleep, brilliant but unspoken arguments rushing through her mind. Tom True had always listened to Prudence.

She heard Drew ready himself for sleep just as he had every evening, removing his coat and boots and cravat, emptying his pockets, winding his watch. His ritual complete, he stood over her. She kept perfectly still until she heard him laugh.

"A sleeper breathes, Meg," he said, stroking her cheek lightly with his fingertips. At his touch, she opened her eyes and glared at him.

"You are still angry, I take it," he said.

He read her feelings too well. She nodded.

"Good night, then." He extinguished the last of

candles, and she heard him stretch out on the floor in the darkness.

An interval passed in which neither the faint hiss and snap of the dying fire, nor the last drops of rain in the gutters and drainpipes relieved the quiet of the room. Margaret tried to hold onto her anger, but the feeling was unfamiliar and uncomfortable. She had chosen to follow him, to learn at last what became of the earl's papers. Though she knew him to be a thief and a traitor, she could not help but wish that he would act with honor and prudence, or forget that only she could remind him of those principles.

Her jaw ached from clenching it, and her neck and shoulders quivered. She could not think clearly, and she had never in her life tried to sleep in such a mood. From time to time she had quarreled with her friend Anne, but the mild stirrings of temper that accompanied such disagreements had always dissolved in laughter. She knew Drew slept no more than she did.

Suddenly the softness of the pillow under her head and the warmth of the thick counterpane over her made her feel petty and mean. She sat up, unsure of what she meant to do, but sure that she must make peace with him.

"Will you light a candle?" she asked. There was no answer, but she heard him rise and saw his shadowy movements against the fire's faint redness. In a minute he had lighted a candle on the small table beside the bed. In its glow his now-familiar features appeared sobered. No teasing sparkle lit his eyes. He turned and stood silently regarding her.

"There is an extra blanket at the foot of the bed," she said. "Will you take it?"

"Thank you, Meg," he replied.

She saw in his eyes that she had surprised him. He didn't move.

"And, here," she said, thrusting a pillow at him, "take this."

His hand came up to accept her offering. "Anything else, Meg?" he asked quietly.

"What else could I give you?" she asked.

He smiled. She knew she had given him an opportunity to embarrass her. But there was no teasing in his voice when he spoke.

"A kiss," he said.

Margaret looked for some playful light in the blue eyes. There was none. He had dropped all fictions between them, all lies and disguises, and she was not safe alone with him. Until this moment she had had to resist only his treason, not his person. His will had compelled them to share many rooms, but kept them from sharing any bed. Now with a word he had evoked her will.

The denial which should have come so readily to her lips, prompted by reason and conscience and prudence, would not come. She should say *No*, and she wanted to say *Yes*. Her throat was tight with the promise of tears. She shook her head.

After that it was impossible for her to look at him any longer. She heard him turn away, and looked up only as he put out the candle. In the sudden darkness he said, "Don't offer, Meg. You will find me only too ready to take everything."

9

THE SUN WAS already low in the sky behind them. At the next village they would stop for the night. Still that last look as she had turned from him two nights before unsettled Drew. By day she rode ahead of him as they made their way from *quinta* to *quinta*, village to village, and he rarely saw her face. Yet in his mind's eye he could plainly see the glossy curls falling over her forehead, the lashes lowered against her flushed cheeks, the luminous shoulder, and the slim, bare arm extended to offer him a pillow. It was a look that every ambitious young woman in London could counterfeit, but in Meg, he knew, the sweet confusion was real.

The fiction of calling her his wife had been a mistake. It had encouraged a developing intimacy of mind between them even as they argued. Then he had held her hand as they listened to the *senhor's* fairy tale of a passion that had outlasted marriage, children, even death. When she had offered her bedding, he had been tempted almost beyond bearing. Recalled to himself, to the bitterness of the circumstances that had incited him to steal Haddon's papers, he had wisely stayed away from her for two days.

But their untrustworthy companions grew more

suspicious and more ready to act against them with
each passing day. He feared nothing for himself; but
could he go on risking Meg's safety? Had he not already given Wellington time to complete his plans for
the spring campaign? Still he was sure that now he
could break the chain that led to the Viper once and
for all. Three days more was all he needed.

Margaret looked around the village they now approached. It was no more than a few dozen buildings
in a hollow, but there was a church and a *tasca* where
they reined in. Their arrival drew the curious and the
enterprising alike, and more than one in the crowd
offered to prepare them a meal and rent them lodging
for the night. After lengthy negotiations carried on
by Esau, they accepted the offer of the man who
owned the *tasca*. Two doors beyond this establish-
ment was a tall, narrow, whitewashed building with
a heavy door set in stone posts and lintel. At the
entrance, Esau passed before them, leading their donkey.

This was a new low in their accommodations, and
Margaret did her best to conceal her surprise. When
the donkey balked at the steep stone steps, Esau
cursed the tired animal in terms that needed no translation and began wielding the crop he carried. With
one of his quick, unexpected moves, Drew inter-
vened, deflecting Esau's arm so that the crop fanned
the air harmlessly. The big man blinked as if he were
not quite sure how Drew had managed it. And Margaret held her breath, for in that sudden compas-
sionate act, the dandy disguise fell away. Then Drew
put a languid hand to the donkey's mane, calming
the frightened animal. With a cheerful command and
a firm slap on the animal's rump, he sent the beast
into the house. He flashed a grin at Margaret and
made a graceful bow, inviting her to enter.

Sure that he meant to enjoy her discomfiture, Margaret marshaled her dignity and her courage and followed the donkey inside. The room with its stone walls and dirt floor clearly served many purposes. There were casks of wine, a cooking area with a tiled hearth, ropes of vegetables and bunches of herbs, and a trough for the donkey. So many smells were mixed in the warm, stale air that it was hard for Margaret to identify any one of them. Across the room a stairway led to the upper stories. As they climbed, Margaret tried to prepare herself for whatever discomforts she would have to face in such quarters. It was her first chance to prove that she meant what she had said at Senhor Fregata's, that she would gladly endure any hardship rather than deceive a decent man again.

Still she was unprepared for the room they entered. It was so small that when their two valises were dropped in one corner there was scarcely room to move about. A patch between the door and window could be crossed in two strides. The only furniture in the room was a narrow bed and under the window a rough table with a pitcher and a basin.

She took a deep, steadying breath and removed her hat and gloves. Laying them carefully at the foot of the bed, she asked for water. While she waited for the water, she hung the jacket of her habit on one of the pegs along the wall, and when the water arrived she began to wash the day's dust from her face as if she were perfectly at home. As long as she kept busy and did not look at him directly, he would not guess her unease.

But he, too, removed his jacket and cravat and then stretched out on the bed, completely filling it or seeming to, so that when she finished her little tasks she felt distinctly awkward. At least his eyes were closed. Perhaps he slept, and she could sit upon the edge of the bed without disturbing him. She knelt and opened her valise, taking from it the book that had enabled her to endure so much awkwardness already. Cautiously she sat against the edge of the bed and attempted to slide onto it without disturbing him, but the bed sagged alarmingly under her and he opened his eyes.

"If you wish to share my bed, Meg, you have only to ask," he said. It was the first time he had teased her in days; and even as her cheeks burned, she felt glad that his earlier coldness with her had vanished. She slid off the bed.

"You know I don't wish to share your bed in the way you are suggesting," she replied, looking about for someplace to sit.

"And what do you know of the way I am suggesting, Meg?" he asked. It was one of those times when she detected a change in his voice, a change that made her aware of the exact distance between them. To stand close to him at such moments was a little like standing too close to a hot fire. Even without the jacket of her habit, she felt warm in the cool evening air. She clutched the book in her hands and thought about what she must do.

"I'll sit upon the floor," she said, and suited her action to her words, crossing her feet and dropping down easily, tailor-fashion. He said nothing. She opened the book across her lap. For some minutes, she sat waiting for a poem, any poem, to catch and hold her interest, but not even the most familiar verse quite made sense to her. Then her gaze was drawn to a black speck on her sleeve. She reached to brush it off, but it jumped. Another speck followed. She looked at the floor; there were dozens of the jumping specks. *Fleas!* She struggled to her feet, sending the book in her lap tumbling, and shook her skirts and brushed at her sleeves. An exclamation of disgust escaped her lips in spite of her best intentions.

Instantly Drew was at her side, urging her to stand still and helping to pluck the tiny creatures from her.

One glimpse of his face told her he had known about
the fleas.

"Oh," she said, pushing him away. "You knew."

"Some men will do anything to bring a beautiful
woman to bed," he teased, and his teasing restored
her composure. He reached to help her again, and
she did not resist.

"I know you don't mean that. It is just one of the
things you say to embarrass me."

"And does it embarrass you?" He reached down
to retrieve her book and she could not see his face.

"A little," she replied, "but for the most part it
distracts me; it makes me forget for a minute the danger and discomfort. That's why you do it, isn't it?"
He had straightened and was holding the book out
to her, but he did not answer. His eyes were night-
blue in the dusk, and there was that expression in
them that she had come to recognize but not understand. Before she could quite fix it in her mind, the
interesting expression disappeared. She took the book
from him.

"Quick," he said, "onto the bed before you attract
a new batch of hungry creatures." He put his hands
to her waist and swung her up on the bed. "This calls
for John Donne, I think."

"John Donne?" she asked. "Oh, you mean 'The
Flea.'" The recollection of that particular poem indeed brought fire to her cheeks.

"Would you prefer Burns' 'To a Louse'? No doubt
there are lice here as well," he said. He was bending
over her, his eyes alight with amusement.

She shuddered, but as she looked up again into the
eyes teasing her, her mind suddenly rebelled. "I don't
believe you," she said, and in the silence between
them she heard the sounds of the village below their
window.

"You are wise not to," he replied, straightening.
"After all, I have more experience telling lies."

"But your lies are not what I thought they were. I do not know why a good man should pretend to be a bad one, but that is what you do. You cannot be the thief and traitor you say you are."

He did not answer but turned away from her so that he looked out the window. "Seeing is believing, Meg. You said so yourself. You saw me take the papers; you witnessed my meeting with Croisset; you see me consort with French agents."

In spite of his level tone she felt she had thrown him off his guard. "Yes, seeing is believing, and this is what I see: I see you laugh; I see your kindness to me, to Senhor Fregata; I do not see—"

A knock on the door interrupted her. It was one of the village boys, announcing in a mixture of English and Portuguese that their *jantar*, the dinner they had spoken for at the tavern, was ready.

"Come, Meg," Drew invited her, reaching for his jacket, "you have an appetite, I am sure."

She did not argue. Her mind was too full of her new idea of him. It was an idea that occupied her thoughts throughout their meal.

They were not alone, but tucked away from the other patrons of the tavern, who stared curiously but did not approach. Her thief was at his most supercilious, rejecting wines and scorning the plain but delicious-smelling dishes put before them. Across from them Esau ate and drank with his usual indifferent steadiness, and Margaret suspected that he was the recipient of the dishes turned away from their table. She never saw Jacob take a bite, for each time she looked at him, he was watching Drew. When they rose to leave, Jacob intercepted them and begged to have a word with "your worship." The false subservience of his sleek looks and voice sent a shiver of fear down her spine, and she clung to Drew's arm.

"Your excellence," Jacob began. He continued in a mixture of English and Portuguese, speaking in the terms but not the tone of deference. At his words, conversation among the patrons of the tavern died, and Margaret felt their stares at her back. She forced herself to concentrate on what Jacob was saying, something about rising early.

"There is no hurry, I think," replied Drew in the languid dandy manner he used before the brothers. He brushed an imaginary speck from the sleeve of his jacket, and Margaret had the oddest feeling she had seen some dandy do just that in London.

Jacob's reply was not perfectly comprehensible to her, but she caught the words for mountains and dawn and the name Vila Real. Their route, their destination, the time of their departure were being announced publicly. Only Drew's grip on her elbow kept her from turning to the villagers behind them. Which of them would carry the message ahead to the Viper, she wondered.

Even as he checked her impulse to turn, Drew was contradicting Jacob. "No, not to Vila Real. This mountain travel grows tedious. I have a mind to return to the river. Tomorrow we will sample the wines of Amarante." He stepped forward, pulling Margaret with him, but Jacob stood intractably in their path. Margaret had no trouble understanding his next words.

"With all respect, your excellence, the wines of Vila Real are superior." The implied threat in Jacob's voice roused Esau.

"What is this, brother?" he called. Margaret turned toward him. His great slack bulk was sprawled in a chair, a woman in his lap facing him, her skirts bunched up about her hips, her legs hanging down on either side of the chair. He stood, allowing the woman to slide down his legs, and came forward still clasping the woman in his rough embrace. "We do as his excellence says, brother. We go to Amarante. Good wines, good trout, good women," he insisted, squeezing the woman at his side and leering at Margaret.

Jacob's expression hardened at his brother's interference, but he said nothing.

"To Amarante, then." said Drew quietly, "at dawn." Jacob bowed slightly and withdrew. As if he were unaware of having aroused the suspicions of an enemy, Drew turned to the proprietor of the tavern and inquired something about the location of the necessary. He accepted a lantern from their host, and he and Margaret set off in the darkness, the conversation in the little *tasca* whispering to life behind them.

Margaret's thoughts stumbled over one another more than her feet stumbled over the dark path behind the tavern. Drew pointed the way to the rude outdoor facility, and they separated. Margaret hardly noticed the humble structure.

Her thief meant to turn away from the mountains where they could most easily meet the Viper. Just at the hour she had conceived a new notion of his goodness, he defied their French-sympathizing escort. She felt almost giddy with hope. She must be right about her thief after all. He could not mean to give the papers to the French. But if Jacob also suspected as much—Jacob, who had been ready to kill them for the papers two days before—then surely their danger was greater now than ever.

That thought hurried her through the necessary actions of the next few minutes and sent her rushing back through the darkness and unexpectedly into Drew's arms.

"Meg, this is something new," he teased, steadying her against him.

"We must not stand here, alone," she whispered back, somewhat breathless with her fear for him, but he did not seem to hear.

Indeed, the suddenness of Meg's stumbling into his arms wrought in Drew one of those changes he experienced more and more often in her company. Caught unguarded against her nearness, he forgot for a moment his intention of returning her to London innocent and heart-whole. He thought only of the rise and fall of her breasts against his chest and the fragrance of her hair. The breathlessness with which she spoke must be a result of her running, but it reminded him of the breathlessness of passion, and he found his own breathing affected.

She was whispering, but the words were an indistinct murmur against his chest. He loosened his hold on her and reached up a hand to cup her cheek. He pushed his fingers into the silky curls at the side of her face, lifting the hair away from one ear so that he might place a kiss there. But just as his lips touched her skin, she spun out of his arms and dashed for a grove of trees at the edge of the field.

He followed an instant later, but she reached the concealing darkness of the wood a few steps before him, and in her black riding habit she had the advantage this time. He stopped at the edge of the wood to listen for her breathing, the snap of a twig, or the brush of her skirts against the undergrowth. There was nothing. Then he heard the crackle of dry leaves from further along the edge of the wood. It could not be Meg. So Jacob would make a move against him here. The thought, which ordinarily would quicken his senses, caused him a sudden painful constriction of the heart as he pictured Meg standing alone and frightened in the dark or Meg in the hands of the two brothers.

Why had she run from him here? At the obvious answer to that question he felt a surge of anger, more at himself for alarming Meg than at her for endangering herself once again. But the anger cleared his mind. He eased his way into the wood, feeling for low-hanging branches. The trees were tangled with vines, perfect for his purpose. When he found a likely branch, he bent it low against the natural curve like a bow tautly strung. Removing his cravat, he tied it around the branch. His scheme was simple enough but took several minutes to accomplish as he paused often to listen for sounds of the other two people in the wood.

The last step of his preparation was to secure the bent branch with a long vine. He turned in the general direction he believed Meg to have taken and paused to listen again. No sound. When at last his enemy moved behind him, he released the bent branch sending it flying upward with his cravat fluttering palely.

Three things happened then in such rapid succession as to seem simultaneous. A shot whistled by overhead; Meg gasped; and his would-be assailant came crashing forward. Under cover of the other sounds, Drew made straight for Meg and caught her. She did not struggle in his arms, but once he released her, clung to his hand so that he had no difficulty in running with her along the edge of the wood back to the village.

All lights were out and the streets quiet in the village as they made their way through the shadows. When they reached their quarters, he paused in the deeper darkness of the lower room to get his bearings. They were both panting from their exertions, but they heard quite clearly the grunts and squeals of Esau and a female companion somewhere in the darkness. As soon as his eyes adjusted to the gloom, Drew made out the stairway and led Meg quietly up it. At their door he scooped her up in his arms, pushed the door open with his shoulder, strode in, and dropped her on the bed. He closed the door, shoved the table across it, and sank down beside her. She immediately scooted away from him toward the wall, and his one thought was to hold onto his anger.

Her thief was angry, Margaret knew, and she suspected he was silent from his effort to control that anger. Without speaking herself, she followed his lead, lying down on her side, facing away from him. She had been angry, too, when he had stood teasing her, ignoring her words, ignoring the danger that threatened. But her anger had yielded to even greater fear when she realized Jacob had followed them and dizzying relief when, after the gunshot, Drew had found her in the woods.

Sleep would be sensible and would allow her to escape the turmoil of her feelings, but the narrow old bed was treacherous, and no sooner had she settled herself than the sagging bed pulled her toward its center so that her shoulders pressed against his back, her hips against his hips. She waited for him to speak, but he said nothing. She struggled against gravity for a few minutes then gave up and lay still. Sleep would come, she told herself, though every part of her felt thoroughly chilled except the two places where her body touched his.

How long she lay, her senses focused on the places where their bodies touched, she could not say, but in time, conceding to herself that sleep was unlikely, she began to think what she must do now that Drew had provoked Jacob into acting against them. She had no doubt that they would find him bowing and smiling in the morning, nor any doubt that he would try again to murder them.

Drew's own words at Senhor Fregata's came back to her. Jacob would not attempt anything until he was sure of the location of the papers. She, Margaret, had been too shy of touching Drew to search his person thoroughly, but Jacob, who had searched their room without restraint, must now believe that the papers were on Drew's person. This then was perhaps her last opportunity to recover the earl's papers, to save the man beside her from the Viper.

If she could get the papers from her thief, then she would have something to bargain with, and she knew what she would bargain for—the truth, nothing less than the truth.

10

MARGARET LISTENED CLOSELY to his breathing for several long moments, assuring herself that he slept. Then she turned toward him, moving with what she hoped would be taken for the restlessness of a troubled sleep should she rouse him. When she had managed at last to turn fully over so that she lay facing his back, she rested her forehead against him and reached over his side with her left hand.

His own arm lay across his chest so she felt first the lower half of the silk waistcoat up to the ribs and then with more difficulty reached over the arm to feel the beat of his heart. She could find nothing, and so, nerving herself yet again, she traced with her fingertips the lower edge of his waistcoat for a place where she could slip her hand between its silk and the cambric of his shirt. Just as she tentatively pushed her fingertips up over the waistband of his breeches, he woke and rolled over toward her, forcing her onto her back and pinning her down with his own weight.

They were both breathing harshly again, and Margaret could not speak. His face was just inches from hers, though hidden by darkness. He lifted himself above her, his arms extended, but his legs remained tangled with hers and his heart beat fast against the hand she had thrown up to hold him off.

"You are angry, I know," she said, "but I had to try for the earl's papers again."

"Angry? You think this is anger?" he asked. He took a long shaky breath. "And what do I do when I'm angry, Meg?" He said her name in a rough way that sent a shiver through her. She shook her head mutely.

She thought about the current of sensation that had jolted her in the second his lips had been pressed against the side of her face. It had been her first kiss, but the exact impression of it was tantalizingly out of reach, for she had not then been attending, her heart pounding with fear. If he kissed her again, she would know more, could think more. But a kiss from him now would be something quite different, she reasoned, something compelling, urgent, in proportion to the way his body strained away from hers.

"Talk, Meg," he whispered, in a voice composed as much of a plea as a command.

"What about?" she whispered back, wanting all at once to touch his face, yet not wanting to remove her hand from his heart and the curious rhythm she felt there. Unbidden, his name came to mind, with a curious longing to say it.

"Your season," he said. "Lady Loosetongue and Lord Leadfeet."

"There's not much to tell," she began. "I didn't take."

"Did you want to?" he asked. "Did you dream of a brilliant season with dozens of beaux?" As he spoke, she felt his heartbeat grow steady against her hand.

"I did not question it," she acknowledged, as much to herself as to him. "My mother thinks a brilliant season is every girl's desire and due. Perhaps I expected too much."

"So you were disappointed when you did not become Miss Reigning Beauty in a fortnight?" His voice had the warm, teasing quality she particularly liked.

"Oh, no. I never expected anything of that sort. I merely expected people to like me," she confessed, finding it easy to admit to him in the dark.

"A natural enough desire," he said. "Why was that too much to expect?" He lowered himself to her side, settling her against him, his left arm under her head, his right hand resting lightly on her arm.

"Because, you see, I didn't really notice people, not as I would have at home. I couldn't think what to say to anyone. They were all so elegant and assured, and I always had something to think of besides the person I was with."

"Go on," he prompted.

"You don't really wish to hear."

His hand stroked her arm lightly, and she shivered an all-over shiver. "Talk, Meg," he said.

"Well, first it was whether my dresses were right, and then it was my hair. And then it was so many things I could not remember what to do with them all—my fan, my eyes, my shoulders, my steps. Mother would signal me from across the room if I forgot something, and so it seemed safer to say nothing, do nothing. Of course, I soon had no partners, and when no one came to my ball . . ."

"No one?"

"No one but my cousins and a few of my mother's particular friends. That's when my mother decided we must do something dramatic, and so she accosted Mr. Brummell, at Almack's."

"With disastrous results, I imagine," Drew said dryly.

"Oh, yes. Mr. Brummell all but said that my mother should advertise me, like some piece of inferior goods."

"And, no doubt, Lady Loosetongue, having no wit of her own, was glad to repeat the Beau's wit at your expense." Her thief sounded angry. "Shall I teach you to see them, Meg, and to laugh at them too?"

"Yes," she said, and so he did, mimicking the lords and ladies who had so intimidated her, and unveiling the follies hidden by glittering jewels and shining silks.

In the morning it did not appear that they were destined to reach Amarante after all. Esau proved difficult to rouse in spite of the severity of the measures Jacob used against him. And when at last the big man staggered out into the daylight, he refused to do anything until he had seen the local *bruxa*, or witch, for a potion and an *oracao* to cure his head. Then it was discovered that one of their horses had wandered off from the field where he had been pastured. When found, the beast was lame. The brothers quarreled at once over who should have the remaining horse. Drew's intervention sent Jacob forth to scout neighboring farms to bargain for another mount. Esau was to complete the packing of their donkey and preparation of the other animals.

In the sudden quiet after so much drama, the villagers returned to their common occupations, and Drew seized Margaret's hand, proposing a picnic. He did not allow her astonished protests to deter him a moment but pulled her after him into the *tasca* where they procured a basket well-laden with bread and oranges and other delectables. Then they crossed the sunny field that the night before had held so much danger, passed through the little wood, now full of cheerful birds, and on up a hilly path, bordered with thyme and rosemary, lavender and rockrose. On an outcropping of granite commanding a view of the road to Amarante, they settled themselves and began to feast on the contents of the basket provided by the tavern keeper's wife.

Her thief half-lay, half-leaned, his back against a boulder. Margaret felt his amused gaze on her as she tore off a hunk of bread or speared an olive or managed a drink from the wine bottle. She kept busy at these small tasks, only occasionally, as a weak conversational gambit, inquiring if he wished for another slice of cheese or drink of wine. He had removed all the airs of dandyism with his jacket, waistcoat, and cravat, and had rolled up the sleeves of a fresh shirt, which bloused loosely around him. Every now and then a puff of breeze blew the sheer fabric against his torso, so that Margaret alternated between a desire to look at him that made her blush and a fear of doing so that made her stare at her hands twisting the folds of her skirt.

"Did no London beau ever lead you down a dark path at Vauxhall, Meg?" he asked.

"No," said Margaret, surprised by the question into looking up and then unable to look away. His golden head was bent, his gaze directed at a stalk of lavender which he rolled between his palms, loosening the tiny purple blossoms and releasing their fragrance.

"No one ever kissed you? No neighboring swain?" He cupped the delicate purple buds in one hand and tossed the stalk away.

She hesitated to answer, so near were they to talking about events between them the night before. She would be at a distinct disadvantage in such a talk, for she had not yet had time to understand his actions or her own feelings.

"No," she whispered.

He pulled her hands free of the folds of her skirt and poured the fragrant buds into them. His sun-warmed touch seemed to awaken all her slumbering senses. "Then my kiss was your first?"

"Does it count?" she asked, speaking the question uppermost in her mind. She raised her cupped hands to her face to catch the scent of lavender.

"Count? Are you going to collect them then, Meg?" He laughed and raised his bright, warm gaze to hers.

"No," she protested at once, "I meant . . . I meant did you do it for the reasons that another man might have?"

"And what would those reasons be?" Now he looked away, and she heard the note of caution in his voice.

"Surely you would know better than I," she faltered, "or perhaps you were only teasing?"

"No, not teasing." He paused and seemed to consider his answer. "Finding a pretty girl in my arms, a girl whose honesty and courage I admire, I took the sort of liberty Lord Leadfeet would no doubt have taken had you given him a chance."

"But you did not do it again when you could have," she said, speaking her thought as it came to mind and wishing it unsaid at once.

"It would not then have been a matter of mere kisses."

"Oh," she exclaimed, and jumped up, unbearably drawn to him, knowing she had come too close, had allowed herself to linger where his person could act like some newly discovered force, drawing her closer still. She strode to the edge of the rock and stood looking out over the valley, seeing nothing.

Margaret had been warned against the charms of Wicked Men almost as regularly as she had been told to stand up straight or to refrain from speaking before her mother's maids. But her mother's admonitions and obliquely told stories of ruined girls had never touched her imagination. The rake who might seduce a girl like herself existed, as far as she knew, only in her mother's mind. And though Margaret understood, in an abstract sort of way, that a woman's body must somehow be involved in her seduction, she had thought till now that the body's role was a minor one, a sort of epilogue to the play. Thus she was appalled at the intensity of her desire to touch and be touched by her companion.

Not that she thought him a thief and a traitor any longer, it was just that she did not know precisely what to think of him. And even if he were the most eligible bachelor of the *ton*, her feelings at this moment were anything but proper.

"Meg?" came his voice behind her. Though she wished to hide her confusion from him, she could not help but turn. As she did so, a movement on the slope above them caught her eye, and she saw Esau step behind a clump of pines. Something in her expression must have alerted Drew.

"Which of our companions is spying on us now, Meg?" he asked with no discernible change in tone though she could sense a wary tautness in his body.

When she replied, he relaxed again. "No need to fear then, for Esau is the blind brother."

"Blind brother?" she asked, very much puzzled.

"Yes, blind. He sees with his stomach and his loins, thus he does not question appearances. Let him spy. He will see only what he expects to see—a man, his picnic, and his mistress."

"What would your mistress, a man's mistress, be doing at this moment?" she asked, surprised at her own daring.

"Complaining," he said repressively. Her question caught him off guard. He knew she did not quite recognize his incipient desire for her, and he meant to keep her from discovering it. At least that had been his intention. He had teased her merely to relieve the awkwardness she betrayed in his presence today. Unfortunately his teasing seemed to encourage her innate frankness. "You are the least complaining female I know, Meg," he finished, hoping to avoid any further talk of the duties of a mistress.

She made a gesture with her hands as if brushing his compliment away. "I mean, what sort of . . . attentions would you be expecting from a mistress, for Esau must expect to see . . . intimacies."

The word was no more than a whisper as her courage apparently failed her, but it reached him just as the capricious breeze brushed his shirt against his skin, and suddenly the desire to feel her touch overmastered him. He tipped back his head.

"Come sit on me, Meg," he invited, giving in to the promptings of that desire. He was behaving like a boy testing his daring. How close to the edge could one go? He repeated his invitation, watching her face.

She came forward slowly as if drawn against her will, hesitated once at his side, and then, gathering her skirts about her, lowered herself gracefully to his lap.

"Bravely done," he whispered, not entirely trusting his voice. He put his hands to her waist and gently pulled her to him. If a tremor shook him, he doubted she noticed, for her gaze was lowered and she was once more twisting the folds of her skirt in her hands.

He pushed her chin up. "Come, Meg, you sat upon your father's lap as a girl."

"Yes," she said, "to hear stories from him, but . . ."

"But?"

"But this is not at all the same." After this confession she hung her head again.

"Shall I tell you a story then, just for a few minutes until our spy goes away?" He pulled her hands free of her skirts and brushed the sweet, clinging buds from her heated palms.

"Yes, please," she said. Her frank gray gaze was troubled, but the thousand messages of his senses to his brain made him incapable of distracting her now.

"Kiss me first, Meg," he suggested, saying what he wanted to rather than what he ought, taking that step closer to the edge, just as he always had as a boy. Pulling her hands forward until they touched the rock behind his shoulders, he forced her nearer to him. He breathed in lavender and thyme and hot pine and the headiest fragrance of all—warm, sweet skin, and his promise to himself to leave her innocent and heart-whole hung in the balance.

It was not at all what Margaret expected. She had thought that seducers were active, pressing their attentions on their passive, subdued victims. But his lying there, giving the control to her, was a powerful form of temptation. All the fleeting impulses to look at or to touch him that she had suppressed, had been able to suppress because each had been a single moment of temptation now conspired against her as she looked her fill.

All lights favored him, she decided, and thought the word for his shining looks was *beauty*, however unconventional an epithet for a man. But more than the beauty of him what tempted her was the unguardedness of his countenance at this moment, as if, though his eyes were closed, his heart was quite open to her. She would kiss him. Caution, a faint voice like her mother's, told her to kiss his brow, his eyes, his cheek, but never the firm, finely drawn mouth. But she thought if she once touched his lips, she might ask him for any truth.

She leaned across the last few inches separating them and pressed his lips lightly with her own. And though she heard his breath catch in his throat and felt his hands tighten around her wrists, the greater wonder was that in bestowing her kiss she should be so shaken, so eager to press not just her lips but her whole self to him. She drew back a little, fighting off the shameless longing. "Tell me who you really are," she urged.

His eyes opened at that, and he looked up at her in bleak silence. He released her wrists. "Is our spy gone, Meg?" he asked. The change in his mood was so abrupt that for a minute she stared at him uncomprehending. Then she glanced at the hillside above them. Esau had indeed gone.

With only a little awkwardness they separated. He

turned from her at once and reached for his waistcoat and jacket while she busied herself gathering the remains of their picnic with trembling hands. When he faced her again with his cravat tied, he seemed to have returned entirely to the aloof role he chose to play for the brothers. His eyes would not meet hers. Neither spoke as they descended the path to the village.

Margaret was free to think, but her thoughts chased each other about so that she could not understand herself. Her body felt peculiar, shaky, as if she had had a fright. Gradually, with the rhythm of their walk, her confusion narrowed to a single, painful contradiction. She must stay as far from him as she could; she wanted only to draw closer. The little breeze, which had teased playfully all afternoon, grew steady and strong, blowing in distant clouds and piling them up overhead so that when they rejoined the brothers and mounted their horses, the sky was dark with threatening clouds.

11

DUSK OVERTOOK THEM on the road. A parley in the
gloom as to whether they should push on or seek
shelter degenerated quickly into a shouting match
between the brothers, with the rising wind snatching
away half their words. Then a traveler coming upon
them from Amarante itself settled the dispute, for,
according to him, they would find no accommodations there. The town, he claimed, was filled with
Holy Week pilgrims. Jacob pressed the man for details. And Drew's translation of the ensuing exchange
filled Margaret with dread. The pilgrims were mem-
bers of a *cofradia*, a brotherhood, journeying to Za-
mora for Holy Week. Jacob's obvious satisfaction with
this information could only mean that they could expect to meet the Viper soon.

Esau, who had been most in favor of stopping along
the road, soon found a deserted barn. Three of its
stone walls were standing, but the roof had fallen in
at one end in a tangled pile of charred timbers. They
entered through a doorless portal in the south wall,
and for a moment Margaret stood unmoving, her senses adjusting to the calm of the interior after enduring
the buffeting wind for so long.

Apparently others before them had used the place

as a makeshift inn. A circle of stones surrounded a pit of ashes, and most of the wood in the place had been pulled down. Esau promptly broke apart the few remaining stall partitions, and soon a fire blazed, casting eerie shadows about the empty barn. Jacob and Drew settled the horses and donkey along one wall near the fallen timbers. The animals were restless with the storm but weary enough to accept the meager provision made for them. The men dragged their saddles to the fire for seats while Margaret set out the bread and roasted meats they carried with them.

Later she thought how pleasant it would be to sit by such a crackling, warm fire out of the wind, talking to her thief, if they had not just passed such an awkward afternoon, and if the scrutiny of the brothers from across the flames were not so disconcerting. Jacob regarded them with cold speculation. And Esau, who ate and drank steadily without glancing at his food, fixed Margaret with a look that made her feel she was likely to be his next course. A sharp word from the thief drew Esau's gaze away from her. With ill-disguised resentment the big man set down his food and shuffled off to fetch a board for the fire. Margaret turned to thank the thief, but he was looking down, trailing a stick across the dirt floor between them. She watched as he drew a square and filled it with intersecting lines. When he began to collect and arrange pebbles and bits of wood, she recognized the figure as a makeshift chessboard and joined in the search.

"How will you distinguish your bishops from your knights?" she asked as he filled more of the squares. "They seem much of a size."

"Ah," he said, "don't you see the bishops' mitres?"

Margaret confessed she did not. "I think it more than likely we will not know our knights from our pawns before the opening gambits are complete."

"Are you afraid to match wits with me then, Meg?"

"Never," she said. "You open." He did so and soon engaged her in play, taking such outrageous risks she was obliged with every move to consider whether he meant to trap her. At length, as she had predicted, bishops and knights, rooks and queens, were hopelessly confused, and they abandoned all pretense of serious play.

Suddenly she was aware, as she had not been in the heat of their play, of the two men on the other side of the fire. The flames were lower, the shadows in the barn more pronounced, and Margaret felt distinctly uncomfortable. The thief's moves, now languid and indifferent, seemed to occupy only his fingers. She sensed that his thoughts, like hers, were on their companions.

He had been turning over a pebble in his fingers and placed it idly in one of the squares. "Your play, Meg," he coaxed. She knew there was no play, but she gave the mock chessboard her attention and deliberately moved one of the small stones.

"Why do they stare so?" she asked lightly, trying to master her growing unease.

Her thief made another meaningless move before he answered. "They are waiting for us to go to bed," he said. It was the sort of remark he had teased her with many times, but the words, uttered in a flat, hard voice, sent the barest shiver through her.

Occupied as she had been with their game, she had not considered sleeping arrangements. It could not be safe for them to sleep in this great open space with the two brothers near. Always before there had been doors to close and lock. Tonight even if they retreated to one of the far corners of the barn, the noise of the storm would conceal approaching footsteps. They might take turns watching through the night, but Margaret doubted either of them could stay awake long. If Jacob had his way, she and the thief would be attacked and overcome without warning.

She must not let the prospect scatter her wits. The brothers had not agreed to kill them, and Esau might yet prevent Jacob from acting. But they would be spared only if they could preserve the fiction that she was the thief's mistress. Until this afternoon they had kept up the pretense by retiring together behind closed doors. Behind those doors her thief had teased her to be sure, but he had never offered her any true insult, rather he had eased her embarrassment in every unfamiliar and awkward circumstance. All the advances in their intimacy had been made before one or both of the brothers.

The thought made her cheeks burn and to put it aside she asked, "Do they mean to attack us?" She heard every blast and rattle of the wind, every restless movement of the animals, every crack of the fire as she waited for his answer.

"I think not," he said, "but they do expect me to make love to you, Meg." He looked at her directly then, holding her gaze with his own, his eyes hot blue, the color of the flame just where it licks the wood.

Her blush of a moment before was a mild sensation compared with those that now assaulted her, a wild fluttering of her heart and a dizzying rush of her blood that rendered her momentarily speechless.

"It is just like you to say that, to put me to the blush," she managed after a pause. "But I know you don't mean to do it, and you are saying it just to make me forget they are apt to murder us."

He laughed. "Or each other, Meg. You have to admit that's a possibility."

They lapsed into silence, which the brooding presence of the brothers soon made uncomfortable.

"You do have a plan, don't you?" Margaret asked.

"I plan to make them think I am making love to you."

She did not doubt the necessity of doing as he said,

and the wisdom to stay away from him was too new, too contrary to the longings of her heart and body to guide her now. But what did she know of lovemaking? Did the man do everything? She had heard young married women speak disparagingly of "the act." What had they said? Whatever the exact movements required, her afternoon with him had proved they would be indecorous and exciting. Surely such acts could only be performed in the dark.

"Will you tell me what to do? I can imagine some things, but . . ."

"What do you imagine, Meg?" he asked, and she heard both amusement and that unsettling change in his voice that awakened sensation in her in the most embarrassing places.

"Shall we be obliged to kiss?" she asked, careful not to look at him.

"Will you mind very much if we do?"

"As we did this afternoon?" She dared to look up. He sat perfectly still as if he could not move, or dared not.

"Not precisely," he said. After a pause he stood and offered her his hand. "Let's make our bed, Meg," he suggested. She nodded, accepting his help.

He gave an order to Esau about the fire and another to Jacob about the animals. As the brothers moved to do his bidding, he and Margaret pulled their saddles, blankets, and valises to the darkest corner of the barn. After they had arranged their bed, he turned away from her and stretched out his arms, holding his greatcoat like a curtain behind which Margaret shed her outer garments and lay them across one of the saddles. She buried herself in the blankets, keeping her cloak tight about her and the largest blanket over her as he had directed.

Though her person was securely covered and she had been near him often in dishabille, she felt the inadequacy of any covers to keep out invading sensation. It was not only that the roar of the wind sounded in her ears, or that the smells of musty hay and charred wood caused her to wrinkle her nose, or even that sharp stones cut into her back—these were surface impressions, easily distinguished from one another. It was his closeness that touched her everywhere at once, overwhelming her senses.

Without turning his back on the brothers, Drew stepped over Margaret and began to shrug out of his own clothes, piling them on top of hers. When he had divested himself of coat and jacket, neckcloth and waistcoat, he sat on the other saddle and pulled off his boots. All his movements were slow, almost exaggerated, and easily recognizable even in the gloom of their corner, except one. In putting his boots aside, he had removed the pistol from his jacket pocket and placed it on the ground next to Margaret's head.

He pulled his shirt free of his breeches and began to undo the buttons. Though this revealing of himself to her was an intimacy greater than any so far, his ease in doing it lessened her uncertainty. And she could not look away as she had schooled herself to do that afternoon. The smoothness of the fair skin, the glowing warmth of it did not surprise her, but the clean structure of him did.

The steel breastplates hanging in dozens of ancestral halls like her own were mere caricatures of these subtle contours, exaggerating the symmetry of swell and hollow that suited this man so well, the swells suggesting power and strength, the hollows, gentleness and vulnerability. Then there was a scar, a slash of whiter skin, shiny and taut across his right side above the band of his breeches.

He knelt beside her on the damp ground, and without thought she reached toward him and drew her finger along the scar. It must be an old wound and could no longer hurt him she knew, but his flesh quivered under her touch and he drew in a breath through his nostrils. She drew back her hand.

In half a minute he seemed to recover. He released the fall of his breeches. That did startle her, but he smiled in his teasing way.

"Turn your face toward our watchdogs, Meg," he said. "You must tell me if they make any move against us."

She nodded and dutifully turned her head toward the brothers. Drew had arranged their valises as a sort of barricade, leaving a space through which Meg could plainly see the two men on the other side of the fire. There could be no doubt they were watching every move her thief made. At her side he lifted the blanket over her and slid under it, but he held himself above her so that she felt only the warmth and the nearness of him.

He began to whisper to her, his lips close to her ear, his breath stirring her hair and sending rills of sensation through her. She wanted to turn toward him, to forget the evils of their situation, but he reminded her not to.

"You have been brave so far, my girl," he whispered. "Be brave for me tonight." Keeping up the flow of words, he nudged her knees apart with one of his own, but he still held himself poised above her.

"Have you been to the theatre, Meg? Have you seen the villain thrust through the heart with a wicked enough looking sword, heard the horrified gasps of the audience?"

"Yes," she answered. She felt herself under some sort of spell invoked by the low, rough quality of his voice.

"But then the fellow stands to take his bow with the others. You had been so convinced of his death a moment before. Then you are relieved. It was an act after all."

"Yes," she whispered, beginning to understand what he intended.

"Tonight," he said, "we convince our audience, but our act will leave you unmarked, Meg, unsullied. Do you understand?"

She could not speak, but nodded her head. Then he lowered himself to her, brushing his body once against her hipbone with a light touch. Her cloak was thick enough, but she felt the stroke of his body and the tremor that shook him. She had to turn to him then. He held himself rigidly above her. His eyes were closed tight, and his breath blew hot and harsh against her chest where her cloak covered her breasts. She put her hands to his fair curls, and gently raised his head. He gave her a smile that did not reach his eyes.

Then he leaned across the inches that separated them. In that first moment, the intensity of his kiss shut out the world beyond their corner, and Margaret let her fingers drift lightly from the sides of his face to his shoulders. Then his weight came to rest upon her, no more than a gentle press, but everywhere at once so that she became conscious of the contours of her body and understood their womanliness. Immediately he lifted his lips from hers.

"Forgive me," he murmured. His kiss changed, and he began a rapid rocking of his hips against hers. The fierce kiss and exaggerated movements meant to deceive their enemies made Margaret feel herself once more an unknowing girl. But she did not shrink from his embrace. Under the show of passion, she felt the honest desire. So, although he pushed violently against her and ground her mouth under his, and though rocks too small to be seen cut her back and her heart was breaking, she simply held him.

Abruptly, he slid off of her, pinning her right arm beneath his chest. He appeared perfectly still as if he had fallen asleep, but she could feel his heart pound, his flesh tremble, and his breath pent in his chest. Bruised and dazed as she was, she knew that his actions had hurt him more than her. She closed her eyes tightly, trying to hold back stinging tears. She could not give way to sobs now without endangering their performance.

When the immediate torment of his interrupted passion had in some measure subsided, Drew raised his head and surveyed the barn. He was not surprised to discover Esau asleep and snoring raucously, but to discover Jacob and one of the horses gone brought him instantly to his feet.

He glanced at Meg. She, too, slept, as quietly and uncomplainingly as she did everything. There she lay on the cold, damp ground in the rough blankets, one white arm outstretched, her dark curls framing her pale, tear-streaked face. How had he gone so far in his game to bring her to this?

He had made love to more than one girl in a barn, before he left home, before Humphrey had caught on to what he was doing and reminded him that he couldn't oblige every lass that fluttered her lashes at him and be a gentleman. But the barns of his youth had been full of fresh hay and healthy animals, and even if the girls themselves had been coarse in their offerings and their demands, he had used them more gently than he had Meg this night.

He couldn't be gentle with Meg and keep to his purpose. Had he been as gentle as he wished to be, he would have stirred her desire and then he would hardly have been able to check his own, wanting her as he did, loving her as he did, as he had for how long without knowing it. He could never have her, and he had known it from the moment in the woods when Ned revealed her name.

He certainly was a fool, but it was time to leave all his games and self-reproaches behind. He would have time for self-reproach later, years for it. Jacob had been gone perhaps ten minutes, no more than a quarter of an hour. How soon would that head start bring him to the village of Amarante and the Viper? Would the Viper elude him at the last?

He dressed hastily, pocketing the pistol once again and Croisset's purse, now much lighter than it had been. He knelt to rouse Meg and could not resist doing it with a kiss. Her eyes opened, and incredibly she smiled. For an instant he forgot his purpose.

"We must leave, Meg," he whispered, recovering his composure. "Jacob has taken our best horse, and I suspect he means to reach the Viper tonight."

"Then you don't mean to meet him?" He heard the hopefulness in her tone.

"No."

"You don't mean to sell him the papers?"

"No." He owed her that much of the truth.

"Why then?" she asked, and he knew she referred to their whole adventure.

"There's no time to explain now," he said.

She needed no further urging. He turned once more and held his greatcoat out to screen her toilet though Esau continued to sleep. When she touched his shoulder, signaling her readiness, he pulled their blankets over the valises and led her through the shadows to the animals. He coaxed the most tractable of the remaining horses out the door and put a bridle on him. Then he mounted and pulled Meg up in front of him.

The fury of the wind was even greater than before, and distant lightning flared against the clouds, but no rain fell yet. Margaret believed they would never find their way anywhere, but, of course, she underestimated her thief. After a dark eternity of plodding into the vicious wind that pierced her cloak and habit, she could see a garish flickering light reflected in the clouds. A few more undulations of the road brought them within view of the town, the outline of its buildings thrown into relief by a seeming blaze in the middle of its streets.

They paused in the shelter of a high wall.

"Meg," he said against her ear, "we have been spied upon; it is time for us to do some spying in our turn. Are you game?"

"Yes," she answered, turning to speak in his ear too.

"I want to see this Viper if I can, not meet him, just see his face and how he operates, whether alone or with others." It was not a question, exactly, but she knew he was asking whether she dared go with him. By rights such a prospect should terrify her; she should argue that it would be prudent to flee. But she could no longer see herself as Prudence in the white cap and silver-buckled shoes. She felt infected by his daring, just as she supposed she had been by all his moods from the first.

"Yes," she said again.

They wound their way among the outermost streets until they came to another road. Even with the wind's roar in her ears, Margaret could hear the rush of water alongside this other road. The thief tethered the horse out of the wind where the animal might crop some grass and led Meg into the maze of streets. The lightning was close enough now that they could hear the accompanying thunder over the wind as they approached the eerie flickering light at the center of the town.

Drew stopped once to remind her of the jewels in her cape and the escape route she must take alone if any accident befell him. He did not allow her to protest. Then, except that he held her hand firmly in his, Margaret would have believed he had forgotten her. They advanced from shadow to shadow, Margaret concentrating entirely on following his lead. Much as she wished to anticipate what lay ahead, she could hear only the wind rattling wooden shutters on the houses and her own heart pounding as wildly within her breast.

In minutes they turned the corner of a street that led directly to the strange, flaring light. The wind now swirled the smoke of torches in their faces. They hugged the walls on the dark side of the street, staying out of the flickering glare, until they could see into the square itself. Margaret could not have imagined the sight that now met her eyes. In the center of a crowd of onlookers was a group of men, dozens perhaps, bearing torches and robed in the brown habits of monks. But they were like no monks she had ever seen, for each face was covered with a tall, pointed hood like a church steeple, blood-red and made the more horrifying by two holes cut in it for the eyes. It was the black, empty eyeholes that made Margaret think of an executioner, the anonymous agent of justice and death. The men were silent, and as Margaret watched, the silent marchers began to circle the square.

"A *cofradia*, a brotherhood. They are as old as the Inquisition," Drew whispered.

"Is the Viper among them, do you think?" she asked, feeling some of her courage drain from her.

He nudged her and pointed. There in the forefront of the onlookers was Jacob, peering intently at the marchers.

The eerie procession passed out of the square, Jacob following. Margaret and Drew went up a parallel alley, keeping abreast of the procession as best they could. They caught up with the lead marchers again at the river, where exposure to the wind's blast threatened the torches. Jacob had disappeared. Drew turned at once, doubling back and pulling Margaret after him until she lost all sense of their direction and stumbled with weariness. He pulled her to him then and held her tightly, allowing her to catch her breath.

Just then they heard voices. Two men were approaching along the cross street. Drew pulled Margaret into the darker shadows beneath a second-story balcony, and Margaret recognized Jacob's voice. Her heart threatened to stop beating, her breath caught in her throat. The two men passed by with quick strides, but a banging shutter above them caused the taller, thinner man to glance over his shoulder. A flash of lightning just then gave Margaret a glimpse of his face. It was as pale as his hood had been red. The skin was stretched tautly over the bones, and a hairless, jutting forehead overshadowed eyes sunk deep in their sockets, a flattened nose, and lips so thin they hardly seemed to be there, a living death's-head.

She wanted to scream her terror but stifled the impulse by pressing her mouth against the warm hollow at the base of her thief's throat. He held her tightly while she shook and trembled against him. When they no longer heard footsteps or voices, he slackened his hold on her.

"Now, Meg," he whispered, "we run."

12

BRILLIANT FLASHES ILLUMINATED the first miles of their journey, revealing a steep, winding road above a river whose waters must be racing, even as Margaret and Drew were, to the Douro below. Then the lightning passed, and an icy, needling rain began. The stinging drops lashed them in waves, penetrating their clothes, treacherously filling up the ruts in the road, and crumbling embankments above them. It seemed to Margaret that the rain was the embodiment of the numbing fear that overcame her the moment she saw the Viper. Only the strong arm about her waist and the warm, steady presence at her back kept her from giving in to her fear. They would be pursued. They must escape.

When the horse refused to go further, they stumbled onward on foot. The rain lessened in intensity and then stopped altogether before first light revealed a village of narrow streets below them on the banks of the Douro itself. Drew went straight to the water's edge. There in an inlet protected from the swirling currents of the storm-fed river were several of the odd craft Margaret had seen days earlier. The sailors, *marinheiros* the thief called them, were huddled around fires on the shore. Welcome smells of food rose in the rain-freshened air. They were a friendly lot, but only one captain, after a consultation with his two crewmen, was willing to accept the thief's money to embark at once with two passengers. Margaret did not need a translation to understand the grave faces of the men and the assessing looks they gave the swollen river.

As the captain and his men set about readying their craft, Drew and Margaret made their way to the house of a port shipper, who, the captain had advised them, might be able to provide dry clothes. Thus Margaret found herself in a small, warm kitchen, its walls hung with bunches of drying herbs. The smell of thyme and rosemary reminded her of their afternoon picnic in the sun, and she felt a little premonition of grief to come as she struggled out of the heavy wet habit she would never wear again.

Her new attire was a loose cotton blouse with a drawstring neckline and sleeves to the elbow. There was a heavy black wool skirt with vertical lines of red embroidery. Both garments had been made for a woman of more substantial proportions, so Margaret was obliged to draw the neckline closed as much as she could and to allow the full skirt to ride on her hips. But there was a beautiful if worn shawl of red and green and gold. She transferred the sapphires and the ring from her finger to a pocket of the full skirt.

Margaret had needed no prompting to hurry at her task, for she much preferred the prospect of death on the river to any encounter with the Viper. In all when they pushed away from the shore, helped in the launching by those sailors who preferred to wait for less hazardous conditions, they had spent less than an hour in the village.

As a child Margaret had often run along the banks of creeks near Wynrose watching the waters carry leaves and twigs. As a young woman she had been on numerous placid excursions on the Thames. But nothing in her past experience prepared her for the sensation of being swept away as powerful surges lifted the boat and sudden turns threw her from side to side against her companion. One of these turns made her conscious that her thief, still in his rain-soaked garments, was shivering. He had ever put her comfort before his own.

"You must get out of those wet clothes," she ventured.

"Will you help me, Meg?" he began, and then the teasing light in his eyes abruptly faded. His voice when he spoke again was full of self-reproach. "No, I don't mean it. I have subjected you to enough impropriety already. Turn away, my girl, for we no longer have your book."

She did as he directed, unable to suppress the feeling that her time with him was slipping away, just as the green banks of the river seemed to slip away from them as they passed by. When she turned back to him, he was attired like one of the crew in loose dark trousers, a rough white shirt, and woolen vest. He handed her his watch and pistol and Croisset's purse. Then he knotted his wet clothes into the discarded jacket and tossed the bundle into the river.

"I don't understand," she exclaimed, for his action recalled her unanswered questions of the night before. "Where are the earl's papers?"

He settled himself on the deck next to her, accepting half of the rough blanket in which she was wrapped, before he answered.

"They are at the bottom of the sea, Meg," he replied. He did not look at her, but what she could see of his face suggested the attitude of a man ready to be condemned or, at the very least, reviled.

"Then you never meant to sell them to the French?"

He shook his head.

"But why did you steal them?" she asked, striving to speak in a reasonable tone.

"I had heard about certain leaks of Wellington's plans and suspected . . . a trusted man. I knew he would be tempted by the particular information in that letter."

"Then you are an agent of the government yourself," she cried, relieved beyond measure.

"No." His denial was vehement, and she felt it like a blow. "No. The man who meant to steal them is my . . . enemy. I acted for personal reasons only. Do not cast me as the hero of the piece. You must not so deceive yourself about me."

She was silent a while, aware that his denial was also a denial of any friendship between them. When she felt she could command her voice, she began to question him again, for she wanted the truth, however painful.

"You stole the papers so that your enemy could not?" she asked.

"Yes."

"And you impersonated this other man when you met Croisset?"

"Yes, as you guessed." At least he was answering her.

"But you did not mean to give the papers over to Croisset?"

"No. I meant to anger Croisset with my demands for money so that he would not deal with my spy again."

"You meant to return the papers?"

"When it was safe to do so. But then I saw that I might take Croisset's place. Croisset is not the top man in the hierarchy. I wanted to follow the chain that led to the Viper to see if I could break it. And then you were there and . . . Croisset's purse." He paused. "For a poor man, having gold to throw down from a fat French purse was great fun while it lasted.

There is just enough left, I think, to buy our way home."

"Home?" she echoed. The word had an oddly hollow sound.

"Yes, home," he replied. He reached for her hand under the blanket and held it between his. "It is time for you to finish your season and find a husband."

"But I do not wish to find a husband among the *ton*," she said quietly.

The hands holding hers shook slightly, but his voice was steady in answering her. "Nevertheless, it is what you must do," he said.

"And you think I shall succeed in winning a man's regard now, after an unexplained absence, when I hardly found dancing partners before?" She meant to make a joke of it, but she had allowed herself to forget London so often and so completely in this other life she had been living that she could not easily think of resuming the awkward role she had briefly played there.

"You underestimate yourself, Meg."

"But I do not underestimate the difficulty of reentering society."

"Your parents will have been advised by the earl to be discreet about your disappearance. We will find out from Ned what has been said, and I will think of something." This last was spoken with a grim determination unlike anything she had seen in him before.

"And you?" she asked, her throat suddenly dry and tight. "Will you resume your old life? Will you marry?" She had been unable to keep from asking it.

"No," was all he said, and she was left to puzzle over which of her questions he had really answered, for the captain came forward to tell them they were approaching some rapids and must secure themselves firmly to the boat.

There were few words between them for the remainder of their river journey. Once, he assured her that if they reached the port-aging sheds at Vila Nova de Gaia on the south bank of the river ahead of their enemies, they would be safe. He did in truth know someone in the port trade who would be able to put them on a ship for London.

After the rapids had been negotiated, they dozed in the sun or watched the changes in the landscape of the shore. Margaret did not wish to move from the position they had taken at the captain's warning, so she continued to lie, cradled between her thief's legs, leaning against his chest. She did not stir or give any sign that she noticed when he stroked her hair and kissed the top of her head. His mood today, if she understood him at all, was one of quiet grief like her own.

As their *barco* entered the wide stretches at the mouth of the river and approached the aging sheds, he returned to his customary quickness of thought and action. Before night had fallen, he had arranged their passage home, and Margaret found herself ensconced with all propriety in a private cabin on a "fishing" ship bound for London. Yet another lie smoothed their way, but she hardly noticed it. She had books and proper clothes and time. She could look back on her adventure and be glad she had lost neither her virtue nor her life, only her heart.

The London to which her thief brought her in little more than a week's time was as foreign as Portugal had been and infinitely less inviting. She felt she had had her bearings briefly at the dockside, but the twists and turns they had taken in the shabby hack defeated her efforts to find any familiar scenes. It was as if they had followed some mole underground and become lost in a maze of tunnel-like alleys whose upper stories approached each other like the sides of an arch.

She hardly knew which of her senses was the most offended by her surroundings. Certainly the eyes could not be pleased by the crowded disorder of the buildings, the cracks, the peeling faded signs, and the layer of greasy soot on everything. The ears, too, were assailed by a din that was forceful, energetic, but without cheer, a collective note somewhere between a groan and a snarl. She was grateful she could give no name to the foul odors that hung in the air.

In their hasty passage from the hack to a tiny room on the upper story of one of the raddled buildings she saw but a few of the inhabitants of the district. These appeared either wretched or predatory, and the language they spoke did not sound like her native tongue. So when the thief told her she must not open her door or venture out for any reason in his absence, she believed him. But she did look out the grimy window cautiously and with increasing frequency, for it was a long day and she had to fight a rising desperation about her circumstances.

It was a most puzzling reaction to events. For now that she was to be returned to her parents within a matter of hours or at most, a day, she felt a sense of some impending catastrophe which she was powerless to prevent. He was going to restore her to her former life, and she would never see him again. All that had happened in Portugal would be no more than a dream, and one moreover that could never be told. There would be no one whose recollection of events and places would serve to strengthen her own.

Already he had withdrawn from her. During their crossing, she had seen him only at the captain's table and had had nothing but the most formal assistance from him to and from her cabin. There had been no hint of impropriety, nor any laughter. She had spent the weary hours considering ways in which they might continue their acquaintance, but she had come up with none. She wished to believe that he felt something of what she felt, that he had come to think of her as a friend, but she had to acknowledge that his actions since they left the river had given no encouragement to her hopes. He had perhaps enjoyed the adventure, but now that it was over he could put Margaret aside and go on. And what would he go on to? She realized she was hardly nearer to the truth about him than she had been when she first called him a thief.

The noise of the street, which had increased in volume through the day, was if anything more raucous now in the waning light, and she was taken by surprise when he knocked. That he was weary was evident in the lines of his face and the subdued color of his eyes. His clothes shocked her more than she wished to show, for he had dressed very much to suit his surroundings in a worn and stained drab coat and ill-fitting breeches over the rough shirt and wool vest he had acquired in Portugal. His boots were unrecognizable as a gentleman's pair for the mud and scrapes. And his eyes told her he knew very well what she thought. He now had the appearance of a thief in all but his face.

The room was no bigger than the one they had shared in the tiny village before Amarante, and though it lacked the fleas, it was otherwise as spare in its furnishings. He placed a bundle, fragrant with the savory smell of meat pie, on the small table and moved to the window, putting as much distance between himself and Margaret as the room would allow. The two actions brought a lump to Margaret's throat.

"Your parents are at Haddon," he said without preamble. "I have arranged a respectable escort for you, so that you may meet them with no impropriety attached."

"Thank you," she said, afraid to attempt more until she could be sure of the steadiness of her voice. She suspected that tears would drive him away from her immediately.

He encouraged her to take a meat pie. She unwrapped the warm bundle and took one of the crumbling pastries. She sat on the edge of the bed with her pie in her lap, breaking off a bite and taking it to her mouth only when she sensed he was tensely waiting for her to do so. As soon as she did, he turned his back on her. The feeling suggested by his movement was so exactly the opposite of her own that the pie in her mouth seemed dry and flavorless and hard to swallow, for it was her greedy wish to see enough of him in this hour to last through all the years of her life.

"Ned reports that your parents have been at Haddon since your disappearance," he continued, as if obliged to offer an explanation. "They have put it about that you became ill there, but the servants' gossip is that you ran away. The earl employed a Bow Street Runner, but the man was unable to trace you beyond Upton, where he found your mare stabled at an inn. I am afraid your mother and father have had a bad time of it. Their unhappiness is yet another charge you must lay against me." He spoke quietly, like a man in defeat, not at all like the bright, laughing young man she knew. The pie in her lap grew cold while she tried to think of something to say to bring back her teasing companion.

"Your parents," he began again, "may doubt you, Meg. Your mother will most likely fear for your reputation and your father, for your virtue. The truth is *you* have done nothing to damage either, but you may not tell them the truth." He spoke now with earnest warning. "Any indiscretion on the part of someone in your father's household could get back to the French. Croisset will come, and the only safe place for you to hide is among the *ton*."

"I understand. I will tell them I ran away, that I found employment as a maid until, just recently, I came to my senses. I will tell them that in returning to them I met . . . met whoever it is you have found to escort me."

"Very good, Meg, an admirable lie for your first independent attempt. It should serve." He turned at last and faced her with wan smile. "Make yourself as elegant as you can. We meet your escort within the hour." He moved toward the door, but she stood, allowing the cold pie in her lap to slide heavily to the floor. She blocked his way, trembling a little from her own boldness, but she could not bear to give up this last hour she might have with him.

"Then I will not see you again," she said, speaking her fear openly, willing him to deny it.

"No," he answered, his face was to the door, and she strained to hear some regret in that low syllable. Was he, like her, afraid to use his voice?

"But does it not seem odd to you that we should have shared such . . . an adventure and then not acknowledge one another? Surely our paths will cross, in London, perhaps. I know you have lived among the *ton*."

"Meg," he said, with some exasperation, "I abducted you, an act that is hardly a basis for . . . friendship."

"You did, of course, but as neither my virtue nor my reputation has been affected, we need not dwell on the fact." The words rushed out in her attempt to convince him.

"I said *you* had done nothing to damage them. I, on the other hand, have done things for which your father might reasonably wish to take a horsewhip to me. Or have you forgotten that night in the barn?" He did not look at her then, and she knew she was blushing.

"You have kept me safe through many dangers and ever put my comfort before your own," she argued, conscious that she must defend him from himself.

"Dangers into which my own recklessness led

you," he said with some heat. "And how would you introduce me to your parents? 'Papa, Mama, here is a man, a sometime soldier, with a talent for lying but no prospects, except for the occasional purse of a Frenchman. Though he abducted me and took advantage of my helplessness to press his attentions on me, we have become great friends. Pray permit him to run tame in your house.'" Somehow in this exchange they had drawn closer, as they had once before in Senhor Fregata's drawing room. . . . She reached out to touch his face.

"Then you have compromised me and ought . . . and ought . . ."

But he flinched at her gesture and stepped back. "If I were a gentleman, Meg, I would be obliged to offer for you, but as I am a rogue and worse, I am under no such obligation, for marriage to me would only disgrace you, not protect you or serve as any reparation for what I have done."

Margaret was silent. She had all but asked the man to marry her, and she was shaken to realize that that was what she wanted. Until just this very moment she had imagined that she merely wanted to continue to have his company. She had thought it would be enough to see him smile at her, to hear him tease, to feel him near. Now she recognized in herself a kind of hunger for him that could not be satisfied. She wanted his love as Ines had had Pedro's, and she was sure that for her as for the Portuguese lovers a lifetime of that love would not be enough. So stunned was she by the strength of her feelings that she did not at first understand his refusal.

"Is that the truth then?" she asked.

"Oh, Meg, do you still have such faith in the truth? Tonight, I swear, you'll learn that the truth can fail you."

"Then you have won. I must lie."

"Your life depends on it, Meg," he said, more gently than he had yet spoken.

"In that then, you do injure me." Some dignity she had not known she possessed allowed her to speak. "And it is no trivial injury as were all the others you charge yourself with, for in lying to my parents, my acquaintance, my future husband, I must go against my nature every day for the rest of my life."

"You will soon be practiced in it," he said.

She gasped at the cruelty. "Do you wish me to hate you then?"

"Yes." He said it without hesitation, and she stepped back from him as if struck. But there was more, and she wasn't sure she heard him right as he passed through the door. "At least, tonight, hate me."

13

THE STREETS HAD quieted when another hack brought them through the dark to a less decayed but still worn building. Outside was a closed carriage guarded by several burly footmen whose livery Margaret thought she should know. Her mind was numb, and her thoughts seemed to stick on such trivial details as if each were a difficult puzzle she must solve. It had required long minutes of concentration to tie the strings of her hood under her chin.

She was still considering the familiar chaise when they entered the building. A butler, she supposed, admitted them, but he was the most singular butler she had ever seen. He reminded her of Esau, and her mind went into another puzzling spin as she considered the butler's odd appearance. The room they entered had pretensions, not the least of which was a gaudy mirror above a great mantel of wood painted to resemble black marble columns.

Margaret's first impression was that they had entered some sort of gentlemen's club, for the room was full of men at their ease, drinking and laughing animatedly. Then she saw that there were almost as many young women present, of varying degrees of

152

harsh prettiness who, breasts bared, were engaged in rubbing, stroking, or playfully tugging whoever was nearest. Her thief was hurrying again, so she hardly had time to take in these details. They went up a flight of stairs, and he knocked once at a door in the dim corridor and entered.

It was a bedroom in a rather florid style with another ornate mantelpiece before which stood a tall gentleman with his back to the door. He wore a bottle-green coat, the quiet elegance of which seemed the more pronounced in such surroundings. That much Margaret observed before the gentleman turned to face them. Then she clutched the thief's arm for support as understanding and recognition cut through the numb fog of her thoughts. The thief's voice confirmed what she had seen at once and added that which she had never guessed.

"Miss Somerley, allow me to present my brother, Lord Durant, Viscount Lyndhurst." The haughty man bowed coldly. "Cyril, this is Margaret Somerley, the baron's daughter. You have no doubt heard of her disappearance from Haddon earlier this spring." Margaret did not hear anything else as she was led to an oddly prim-looking gilt chair, for she was fully occupied in absorbing all that was meant by the connection and the contrast between the two men.

Here in this elegant lord were her thief's features, but with a coldness, an immobility, a sharpness that robbed them of true beauty and any joy. The brothers were enough alike that the thief, Andrew Durant, as she must now think of him, had been able to impersonate Cyril at the meeting with Croisset, and yet they were unalike. The viscount was taller and thinner of face and body, and these proportions, while distinguished, were less handsome. The hair was a light brown with only hints of gold. The eyes were blue perhaps or gray. In short, Cyril Durant was a man whose appearance must please until one saw his brother, then one was conscious only of the flaws in the older man's countenance, of the degree by which the whole fell short of the other's perfection. And, observing those cold features, Margaret knew for a certainty that Cyril Durant hated the younger brother who so eclipsed him even in rags.

"Do you wish to explain yourself, brother?" the viscount asked. "In spite of your choice of meeting place, I do not think you called me here so that we might indulge in some sort of fraternal bacchanal." He made a lazy gesture toward the floridly draped bed. It was the sort of movement the thief—Drew, she corrected herself—had mimicked perfectly.

"No, it's an awkward circumstance, Cy, but I find I must apply to you for help. You are in a position to aid Miss Somerley, a damsel in distress, and I could hardly bring her to you in Bruton Place."

"A baron's daughter? Not your usual style, brother," replied the viscount, raising a quizzing glass and examining Margaret through it. He let the glass fall. "My brother, Miss Somerley, is a thorough democrat. He prefers the company of stable hands to that of his own family and would rather make love in a barn than a bed. He has never understood what he owes our name."

"*Owed*, Cy, as it is not my name any longer."

"Just so, brother. Does it hurt you much?"

Margaret gasped. There was a pause in which she recalled the pained fragments of their conversation whenever she touched on her thief's family. The taut scar across his side was the least of his wounds.

"Yes," he admitted, and his brother smiled. "But you were not satisfied with that, Cy," the younger man continued. "You wanted to embarrass the old man further. I had thought my fall from grace would have sated you."

"It would have, brother, but, you see, the old man still grieves for you. Of course, he hides it from the world. He made a great show of stripping the house of your things, you know, your portrait, your clothes, your horses, your dog. All signs of you are gone. He never speaks your name. Indeed, to please him, no one speaks of you these days. I have not had to endure your praises for two years."

"So I ask again, Cy, why were you not satisfied?"

"Ah, but do you know what I discovered? I discovered he wears your portrait on a chain around his neck, like some green girl pining for a lost love. Not my mother's picture—he buried her—your picture."

"Would you like me dead then, Cy?"

The viscount shrugged. "If you should suffer in the dying."

"It can be arranged," came the answer.

"I am interested," was the cool reply. Neither man had moved. The elegant lord still lounged against the mantel. The young man in rags leaned as easily against the door. Yet it seemed to Margaret as if the fencers had just removed the tips from their foils.

"You see, Cy," said the younger man, "I have met your man, Croisset. I did not give him the papers, however, but knocked him on the head, stole his purse—" Here, he dangled the empty leather purse. "—and spent his gold without giving fair return I'm afraid." An oath escaped the otherwise composed Cyril. "And worse, his fellows have been chasing me about Portugal this past fortnight instead of following Wellington as they ought to have been."

"Still playing games then, brother?"

"Exactly, Cy, and that's what I wish to propose to you tonight—a game. Winner lives, loser dies."

"Games are your forte, not mine. You can't be serious."

"Oh, but I am, and you can't avoid this game, Cy. In fact, you are already playing. You see, the French believe *you* met Croisset, deceived him, stole his purse, teased the Viper with information you did not deliver and must still have. The French don't know *I* exist. When Croisset comes, he will be looking for you."

"I do not see the game in it, brother. What move is there for me to make?"

"Of course, it could be a different game. We could work together to expose Croisset and disrupt his network." Margaret heard the faint hope in the words. They were answered by a barely perceptible shake of Cyril's head. "Then you do prefer to play my game?"

"It seems I have no choice." Cyril's coolness was replaced by distinct irritation.

"You will like it, Cy, for it's an easy game for you to win, a matchmaking game." The viscount gave something like a snort. "You have only to restore Miss Somerley to the *ton*, to offer her your support in her reentry into society." As Cyril turned his cold gaze on Margaret, the younger man continued. "When an announcement is made in the *Morning Post* of her betrothal to some eligible gentleman, I will give myself up to you, Cy." *No*, thought Margaret, but Cyril's gaze kept her from speaking. "You may offer me to the French, or, if you prefer a more public execution, you can expose my traitorous acts to English justice."

"You paint an attractive picture of victory, brother, but might I not lose?"

"Yes. The French might find you first."

"The thought occurred to me. Suppose Miss Somerley is nice in her requirements of a husband and cannot be satisfied with any of the proposals she receives?"

"But you must put charming men of good birth in her way and enlist the aid of her parents, who are most eager for their daughter to be advanced in the world."

"Could I not simply marry the girl myself?"

"Unsporting, Cy. Besides, the girl won't have you. She's not fond of me above half, but she's plagued with a conscience that wouldn't allow her to do me in so quickly." Unexpectedly the viscount whirled on Margaret, seizing her roughly by the chin and turning her face to the light.

"What is she to you, brother? Little innocent that she seems, is she your cast-off?"

"Miss Somerley is nothing to me," came the answer with an indifference that Margaret found convincing whether the viscount did or not. "A chance-met acquaintance. As you said, she is not in my style, hardly a girl to roll in the hay." Margaret met Cyril's gaze unflinchingly, for his cruel hold could not hurt her as his brother's words did. For a moment she doubted the viscount would believe his brother, but then he dropped his hand from her chin and turned to the younger man.

"And Miss Somerley's conscience is not too delicate for this game? We may trust her discretion?"

"I admit, there's a bit of awkwardness to Miss Somerley's position, for someone with a conscience, but she can hardly refuse your help if she wishes to be restored to her family, and it is not in her power to say how I should repay you for your gallantry. Besides, she has a most embarrassing absence to conceal from the *ton*."

"Well, then, little brother, I will play your game, but remember—Miss Somerley will be within my reach should you play me false." He offered his arm to Margaret with perfect civility, as if their whole bizarre agreement were the most usual sort of converse between two gentlemen. "Miss Somerley, will you accept my escort to Haddon?"

"Gratefully, my lord," she lied. Drew Durant stepped to one side to allow them to pass, and Margaret meant to do so with her pride intact at least, but there was a moment's delay at the door itself as the viscount reached for the handle, and she had to look one last time at the golden-haired man in rags.

His gaze met hers and seemed to challenge her, as if to say, *How do you like the truth*?

"Good evening, Miss Somerley," was all he said.

"Good-bye, Mr. Durant."

14

N OW THAT HE had done it, Drew thought he might
congratulate himself on the manner in which he
had let Meg go, but unaccountably he felt it necessary
to sit down first. The gilt chair she had so recently
occupied would not do at all, but there was a scroll-
armed couch on the other side of the mantel if he
could make it so far, and a companion table held a
brandy decanter and glasses. He steeled himself for
the effort and had unstoppered the decanter and begun to pour before the trembling started.

He spilled most of the first glass. Indeed he found
the trembling uncontrollable until he had managed
to imbibe at least some portion of several glasses of
the inferior brandy. But the shaking would pass. It
was merely the inevitable reaction to the rigid restraint he had imposed upon himself during his time
with her.

In the beginning of their adventure it had been no
more difficult than other restraints he had been learn-
ing since boyhood. One learned not to slide down
banisters, not to gallop one's horse in town, not to
respond to every woman's glance, not to speak one's
feelings. And at first he had told himself he was
merely amused, merely stirred because he had been

celibate so long. But their picnic on the rock had awakened some realization in him of how deeply he had come to feel. The sweet provocation of her kiss had run through him like fire along a fuse, and it was fortunate that she had spoken and recalled him to himself.

Then in that barn on the road to Amarante he had been caught by the necessity of keeping up their deception, knowing if he did not, he risked having their guards agree to kill them there. What a mockery of his love and desire that had been, and how impossible to be in her company alone ever since. On their return voyage he had had to struggle constantly with images of entering her cabin and taking her into his arms. If he had once crossed that threshold, he would have made her his. There would have been no more choice in the matter for either of them, and he had no right to take away her choice. So each day he had persuaded himself that he could hold out against temptation one more day, and somehow the days had passed.

Now he would be free of that particular agony, for the trouble with deciding to be good or honorable, which he had never noticed before, was that one had to repeat the exercise of will endlessly, whereas when one yielded to temptation, the thing was done. He had arranged it so that she was out of his reach. Within a few weeks she should be safely wed. And then he would hardly mind dying at all.

Still a doubt nagged at him, demanding he drown it in more brandy. He knew that she was not indifferent to him, that he had hurt her tonight. He might have touched her girl's heart and stirred some longing in it. But she had heard his name there in the wood, just as he had heard hers, and for all the hundreds of times her name had been on his lips, because he couldn't help saying it, she had never once used his.

She had suggested they continue their acquaintance

only when she was ignorant of his true position. Surely tonight she had seen the impossibility of any connection between them. This quarter of London had shocked her as he had intended it should. He had shocked her, appearing like one of the denizens of the place in the used clothes he had purchased on Monmouth Street.

If she had come to London two years before when he had still been his father's son, he might have courted and won her. Second sons of earls might marry baron's daughters. But she had come too late. *Too late* . . . The words recalled the wisdom of the Portuguese. *It's too late, Ines is dead.* He understood Senhor Fregata's irony. His Ines, too, was dead, or as good as dead. He would never be the fool Prince Pedro had been, exhuming his love. Meg was lost to him; so be it. But he would have just one more glass of brandy to help him accept the fact.

The carriage that had puzzled Margaret when they entered the bawdy house had been there for her, of course. The livery was that of the Earl of Haddon, and the footmen were every bit as solicitous as they ought to have been when the viscount handed her into the chaise. There was a shy little abigail huddled in one corner, whom the viscount introduced as Nancy. The proprieties thus observed, the occupants of the well-sprung chaise lapsed into silence as soon as the horses began to move.

The numbness that had overcome Margaret earlier returned. Drew had been right about her. She had put all her faith in the truth, and in love. She had been so sure that the truth would vindicate him, would prove him as good and honest and worthy as her heart believed him to be. But the truth was that he did not love her, and that some time long before they met he had put himself beyond the pale. Numbness was not enough; she wished for oblivion. How-

ever, it was not she who dozed, but the young serving
girl.

Then Margaret became aware of the close scrutiny
she was receiving from the viscount. When a bump
in their otherwise smooth ride caused Nancy's reticule to slide from her limp hands, revealing how
sound asleep the girl was, the viscount bent gracefully
to retrieve the small bag and placed it on the seat next
to Margaret. She was not surprised to hear him speak.

"You have been gone above a fortnight, Miss Somerley. You look well, considering the dangers and
deprivations a gently bred young woman might find
herself exposed to among strangers."

"Thank you, my lord," seemed the safest reply.

"Just when in the course of your adventures did
you meet my brother?" His use of the word *adventures*
alarmed her, for she did not wish to be at this man's
mercy, as she would be if he guessed even a part of
the whole.

"I never knew your brother before tonight," she
answered, thinking how true it was and how much
of a lie it sounded.

"Ah," came the reply. "Well, my brother was ever
an impulsive young man." He paused. "I have no
doubt he loves you, Miss Somerley."

If Cyril Durant meant to disconcert her, he very
nearly succeeded. "You mistake the matter, my lord,"
she said, the pain of it allowing her to speak evenly.

"Do not bother to deny it, my dear," he said un-
pleasantly. "You see, along with the excess of beauty
with which nature favored him, my brother is also
favored with an excess of nobility. Whatever satisfaction it gives him to put me in this position, his aim
is your happiness."

"Sir," said Margaret, uncertain of her ground with
this man, "you imagine a connection between myself
and your brother. I simply wish to be restored to my
parents and now find myself a pawn in a game not

of my choosing." She hoped she spoke with just the degree of indignation to make him believe her. It did seem for a moment as if he would allow their conversation to lapse. Then her hopes were dashed.

"No, Miss Somerley, it won't do," he began. "My brother wants your happiness so very much, he offers me what I want most in order to ensure it. This is no quixotic gesture on behalf of a chance-met acquaintance."

It took considerable effort to meet the unwavering gaze directed at her. "You see what you expect to see, my lord," she said, unable to quite deny his words as they evoked the first hope she had felt in days.

"Your courage and your loyalty do you credit, Miss Somerley, but you need not fear me. Though the easiest way to cause him pain would be to hurt you, I do not mean to do it. My brother is always bravest, always at his best when he is most hurt. Unfortunately, my brother's nobility of character brings out the worst in me. Everyone admires him, so I cannot. Everyone loves him, so I cannot." He stated the fact regretfully, but Margaret did not allow herself to hope that he would change his mind about the game. His hatred for his brother was obviously of too long standing.

"I mean to play this game, my dear," he assured her. "Of course, I will cheat."

Margaret gasped, and the viscount laughed coldly. "Do not be so alarmed, Miss Somerley. He expects me to cheat. He is not stupid, my brother. And it frees you, really. You may marry whom you please or not marry. The announcement in the papers will not be his death sentence after all, for I mean to find him before his foolish game comes to fruition."

Margaret was grateful to reach Haddon almost immediately after this revelation of the viscount's character. She did not think she could endure another moment alone in his company.

The next hours went by in a blur. No sooner had she and her escort entered the hall than her parents appeared in quite rumpled states of undress, looking both older and smaller than she remembered, though such a thing could not be.

"Oh, Margaret dear," her mother cried. "We feared such dreadful things."

"Mama, Papa, forgive me," she said, stepping into her father's open arms. "I never meant to cause you such distress. It was only that I didn't wish to disappoint you anymore, so . . . I ran away."

"My dear," said Lady Somerley, now reaching to embrace Margaret, "how could you disappoint us? You are so lovely and so clever, and if only we had not left London, I know you would soon have had more beaux."

Margaret caught her father's glance and refrained from any contradiction. "Perhaps in time, Mama, I will meet some fine country gentleman at an assembly in Bath."

"But your season, dear. I promised you such a lovely season, and it has all come to nought."

"Now, my dear," said Margaret's father to his baroness, "time enough tomorrow to worry about her future. Tonight we must celebrate our prodigal's return."

Margaret then gave herself over to their embraces and dried her mother's tears, for she had none of her own. She endured their grateful praises of the viscount, whom they could not thank enough, but she was glad of the earl's suggestion that they retire to the privacy of her mother's apartments.

A cold collation was sent up from the kitchens, and she made a show of taking a little of this and a little of that, though she had no appetite for any of it. Her parents asked many questions, but fortunately did not press for answers, seeming content merely to gaze at her and touch her. She sensed that their greatest need was for this touching, to assure them that she was truly back, so she allowed herself to be squeezed and petted into the small hours of the night. She did not object even when her mother asked that a couch be made up for her there in the same room. Her parents had been most hurt by her absence, and though she could not be their child in quite the way she had been, she could assure them of her love.

The young man with red hair gazed wonderingly at the splendors of his first London brothel. When he entered the main salon, he hoped to glimpse some of the ladies' charms, but the opulent room was empty so he made his way directly, if somewhat reluctantly, to the upper room where he had been told he would find the customer he was looking for. The bed in the designated room, with its exotic golden drapery, was so exactly what he had imagined it would be, that he lost himself momentarily in luxurious fantasies. Then his gaze took in his friend sprawled on a fancy couch, and he went at once to the wreck of young manhood there.

"Drew, Drew," he urged as he shook the sleeping gentleman's shoulder, "you can't stay here. Cy will be looking for you already."

"Ned?" the other mumbled. "Did he take her to Haddon?"

"Aye," said Ned. "It's the talk of the kitchen how her mama and papa wept at her return. The chit never shed a tear herself though."

When the still-recumbent young man showed no inclination to move, his redheaded friend shook him again.

"Come on, Drew, it's near dawn. Let me help you up."

"Sure, Ned, best of friends." Some further repetitions of this exchange were necessary before the golden-haired man on the couch at last opened his blue eyes and swung himself into a slumped sitting position. Then there was an awkward moment when the drunken man stood too quickly and leaned heavily against his friend, nearly toppling them both. When they were both reasonably steady on their feet, they began to move toward the door with exquisitely slow steps. They had not progressed far, however, when the golden-haired man clutched his friend abruptly.

"The slop bucket, Ned. I'm afraid I'm going to cast up my accounts."

It was several minutes before either of the pair spoke again, but then the golden-haired man seemed more in command of himself.

"I owe you, Ned," he said quietly.

"You don't owe me. Doing it up too brown, Drew," said the other.

In the bleak gray street below they parted with a final exchange.

"You got the lodging I arranged?" asked Drew, shaking a bit in the cold air.

"Yes, I got it, but the whole idea's stupid, if you ask me."

There was no immediate answer. "Just watch her," came the reply at length. "See that Cy doesn't hurt her and the French don't get her. I'll find you whenever I want a report." He began to walk off with a stride that was amazingly steady. "And Ned," he called back, "get a hat that covers that hair."

15

I T WAS INEVITABLE that Lady Somerley should begin
to think of London again within a few days of her
daughter's return. She found in Cyril Durant a sympathetic listener. The viscount concurred exactly in
her judgment and seemed to have taken a most grat-
ifying interest in her daughter, proposing that he escort Margaret to all her engagements until the girl
should feel comfortable in going about again.

Lady Somerley congratulated herself on her own
discretion in refraining from the mention of Margaret's earlier embarrassments. If this fine son of their
dear friend found Margaret charming, she would not
encourage him to think otherwise. He had mentioned
Almack's, and what a salve it would be for her
wounded pride to return to that scene of former humiliation with such an elegant and eligible escort. No
man would then overlook her daughter. She resolved
to attend the first Wednesday that a suitable gown
could be made up for Margaret.

Margaret found that Almack's, like her parents, had
shrunk in her absence, and she was inclined to laugh
when Cyril Durant introduced her to the young men
of his acquaintance. The irony of their eagerness to

meet her followed by their quite genuine surprise that they had done so weeks before afforded her a sort of bleak amusement.

She smiled and dipped gracefully into a curtsy before Brummell, then moved easily into the opening set with the viscount. As naive and generous as she had been during her first foray into society, she would have attributed society's cordial welcome to her elegant new gown of a blushing shade of satin. But a teasing voice in her head said something about the dreadful susceptibility of the *ton* to a few fashion-setters. She almost turned as if she could catch a glimpse of him somewhere in the crowd. It unsettled her for a moment, but she recovered her poise. It would never do to think of Drew Durant at so public a moment, though his words about their class had never seemed truer. Her worth among the *ton* was being reassessed because the fashionable viscount appeared to value her.

After standing up with Cyril Durant for the first set, she had no lack of partners. She meant to notice each one of these potential suitors, to note their charms and fix their names firmly in mind. It was a matter of pride merely, not inclination. She would do what a young woman of her station was obliged to do—she would please her parents. But she found herself distracted or perhaps abstracted, as if she were listening to the conversation of her partners from a great distance. One young man with a pleasingly cheerful countenance had trod mercilessly on her satin-clad toes whenever the movement of the dance allowed, but she scarcely noticed until, quite suddenly, she woke up. She had not realized she had been asleep, but she had been ever since the dreadful night of her return to Haddon, asleep in all but the most literal sense.

"My lord," she said, having forgotten his name but

assuming there was some sort of title, "do you know Andrew Durant?"

He blinked at her. "Yes. No. That is to say, he was disowned, you know—not supposed to speak of him to a lady, beg your pardon."

"But it was I who spoke, Lord . . ." She almost called him Leadfeet. "Why is Mr. Durant not spoken of? What did he do?"

"Excuse me, Miss Somerley, can I get you some refreshment?" He hastened away without waiting for her reply. Suddenly the room was peopled with those Drew had mimicked. Of course, he had been one of them, had been liked, loved, she was sure. What could have happened to make him such an outcast? Cyril Durant was admired, fawned on, imitated, but he was not loved. What had Drew said in that terrible meeting in the brothel? Had the viscount caused his younger brother's disgrace?

"So, Miss Somerley," came Cyril's voice beside her. "You have had a triumphant return. Your mother is beaming upon us with the light of a hundred candles in her smile."

"I have not yet received any offers, however, my lord," replied Margaret coolly.

"There is no need for undue haste, my dear," said the viscount. "I do not wish you to make a choice you would regret, merely to save my life. Besides, I expect to find my brother any day now. Then you need feel no concern at all in the matter."

"Are you so certain of success?" she asked. In the week or more since Drew had left her, she had accepted the loss of him in the numb way she had accepted everything offered to her. Drew had said she was the least complaining of females. But now she realized she had acquiesced too soon. The circumstances revealed to her that night had been only a part of the truth, not the whole. Whatever disgrace he had suffered, Drew was not dead, and it was not too late to act to save him.

"My dear," said the man at her side, "what a lovely, expressive face you have. Do not imagine that you can save him. You would be wiser to consider yourself his widow. It will help you choose your next love more prudently."

Anger, as unfamiliar a feeling as it was, sustained Margaret through the next hours. Though she was impatient with all the ritual and formality of an evening at the holy of holies, the temple of the *ton*, where suitable connections among its elite could be arranged, she would not give Cyril Durant any further satisfaction from outward shows of her distress.

In the privacy of her own bedchamber she gave way to the tears she had been holding back since that day on the river, and her last thought, the one that hovered lightly in her mind before sleep, was that Drew Durant had somehow awakened all her passions.

In the morning, however, she was resolved to think rather than feel. She had an adversary as ruthless and determined as either Croisset or the Viper, and she did not know how much time she had to act against him or—what to do. By the time she had dressed and breakfasted, she had decided that her first object must be to discover the truth about the earl's second son.

But a fruitless day and evening of talk and dancing passed away under the watchful gaze of the viscount. The subject of conversation nearest the one she longed to introduce was a tedious account of the hardships of the Peninsular War and the details of Wellington's brilliance. The next day a new problem arose to plague her. She was being followed, or rather watched.

It was a feeling she had learned to recognize in Portugal, a disturbing sense of someone's presence that traveling with the ever-watchful brothers had taught her. When she thought about it carefully, she realized that she felt it only in the environs of her own home in North Audley Street. If the carriage once turned the corner, it was gone. By Saturday she was sure she could identify the feeling with the presence of a figure that occupied more or less the same corner as she came and went. The figure was that of a man, but beyond the gender she could tell little. He had a long coat and a squashed coachman's hat pulled low, obscuring his features.

She tried to think rationally about the mysterious figure in spite of the fear his presence evoked. Perhaps Cyril Durant was taking precautions against some action on her part. Perhaps he believed his brother would come to her. Then again, perhaps the French had already traced them this far, or, irony of ironies, had connected her with Cyril, as she was so often in the viscount's company. She felt powerless again, as she had on the voyage from Portugal. Events were closing in on her. Then unexpectedly the weather took a blustery turn, changing all her prospects. As she stood in the window of the morning room, looking out at the mysterious watcher, a gust of wind blew his hat off, revealing a handsome, youthful face and unmistakable red hair.

She quickly decided that the best plan for capturing Ned was the simplest. So that very afternoon, in spite of the gusts of wind, she pleaded a need for fresh air and exercise, arguing that as rain must come soon, it might be her last chance for a walk in days. She gathered her cloak and hat and reluctant maid and set out for the park, noting with satisfaction that Ned followed them at once. Impatient as she was to talk to him, Margaret forced herself to keep a decorous pace as far as Grosvenor Square. She instructed Betsy in her plan, keeping the reasons for it to herself. When they turned onto Upper Brook, she hurried a bit so that they were well ahead of Ned when he reached the turn. She could almost sense his dismay when they turned right at Park Street. Her trap was set, and she waited eagerly for Ned to come hurrying around the corner.

He must have sprinted the distance because he was quite winded when she stepped into his path not above a minute later. Then before he had time to register his shock, she accosted him.

"Who sent you, Ned," she demanded, "and why are you following me?" He backed away, still breathless, and she feared he meant to turn tail and run so she rushed into further speech.

"Ned, do you want him to die?"

He stopped then and glared at her, still laboring to catch his breath.

"You and I are the only ones who can save him," she continued.

"You?" he exclaimed, putting a great deal of doubt into one syllable. "You save him? Small chance of that. Because of you, he's living in some rat hole in the Holy Land, doing Lord knows what."

"You've seen him," she cried. Ned was ready to deny it. "You have seen him," she insisted. "How is he?"

"Well enough, no thanks to you," came the reply.

Margaret studied him briefly, determined not to lose what seemed her only possible ally in the attempt to save her love.

"You are only cross because you are tired and you got caught," she said. "This game was not my idea, and he didn't give me any more choice in it than he has apparently given you."

His breath at last recovered, Ned grinned at her. "No, I guess he wouldn't."

She smiled back. "Will you follow me home then? Just as you would have, and then come round to the stables. For we must talk."

"Now, miss," said Ned warily, "I don't know what

you're thinking. But he won't like it above half that you caught me, and he certainly wouldn't want me to talk to you."

"But Ned," she said in her most reasonable tones, "if we don't talk, he will die."

"Lord," said Ned, acquiescing with the air of a man abandoning himself to disaster.

It was necessary to calm Betsy's fears at such uncharacteristic behavior on her mistress' part and to promise extreme caution and decorum in all her dealings with Ned. And she had to distract the disapproving Betsy further with several small tasks in order to slip the sapphires and ring into her reticule unnoticed. Still other forays into lying were necessary before Margaret could escape the house for the stables. It occurred to her that Ned's cross humor was probably a sign that he was hungry and weary, so she inveigled a tankard of ale and a slice of cold meat pie out of Cook. Then, as it had begun to rain, she strapped on her pattens and wrapped her cloak about her.

Though she was damp and chilled when she reached the stable, the rain proved to be a blessing, for no one came to request a mount and the grooms and stable hands, given a respite from their labors, had gathered to roll dice and tell tales. As there was no mistaking Ned's hair, she thought it wise to tell her own groom who Ned was. Beyond that she concocted yet another flattering fiction about intending to show Ned some trick of the Somerley stables that he might employ for her when she was at Haddon.

Thus they were quite ignored and took a pair of stools to an empty stall. Margaret offered Ned the refreshment she had brought, and he took it warily. The stubborn cast of his features told her her task would not be easy. She allowed him to eat and drink without interruption, listening to the rain patter softly against the stable roof, wondering how to begin.

"Have you always lived at Haddon, Ned?" she asked, as if he were a guest in her mother's yellow salon. She could tell he wondered at her tone, but apparently he saw no harm in answering her question.

"Yes."

"Then you have known Drew a very long time?" There was a kind of forbidden pleasure in speaking his name at last. "Was he much like he is now?"

Again Ned seemed to consider the wisdom of answering her. Then he grinned. "Just like," he said. "He was always a sudden fellow, and he always did everything better than anyone—shoot, ride . . ." He clamped down on his own words of praise.

"Better than Cyril?" asked Margaret.

"Way better," Ned confirmed.

"Is that why Cyril hates him so much?" she probed.

"That and . . ." Ned stopped abruptly and glared at her. She had the distinct impression that he had just become aware of where her questions had been leading him. "If Drew didn't tell you himself, he sure as fire wouldn't want me to tell you."

"Ned," she said, feeling her patience dissolve, "for days I have been left to wonder why I was being watched and by whom. This afternoon I have lied to my mother, my maid, Cook, and Thomas, and now I want the truth." Ned's face remained set in stubborn lines. "Ned," she warned, "he will die."

"Devil take it, miss, will you stop saying that," he pleaded, jumping up and pacing the narrow stall.

"But I am afraid of it every minute," said Margaret in a small voice.

"Lord," said Ned. He sat down again, and ran a hand through his startling hair. "It's mostly kitchen gossip I have," he continued. She gave him a look to let him know she would brook no more delays.

He took a steadying breath and plunged into his story.

"Drew was wounded at Badajoz and got some fever, and they sent him home in June of '11. So he stayed the summer, healing, and helping the old man with his papers. All the Haddon folk fussed over him like he was some kind of wonder, but he wasn't really . . ." He stopped and seemed at a loss for words.

"Content?" Margaret supplied.

"That's it. He couldn't ride, and he didn't have any of his friends. There's me and there's Humphrey, but I'm a slowtop to him, and Humphrey's an octosomething."

"An octogenarian?"

"Aye," he said, looking at Margaret with some respect. "So when fall came and the earl went up to London, Drew went too. I think he must have burst on London. Leastways I think the ladies there must have gone mad for him."

"Have ladies always liked him so much then?" Margaret asked, afraid she knew the answer.

Ned shrugged. "County girls have. I couldn't speak for the ladies. But in London there was this Miss Chilton. She was something else, everybody said, an out-and-outer, with a fortune, too. 'Angel-face,' they called her. I guess both Drew and Cyril paid her some attentions."

"Oh, no," said Margaret.

"Well, all the gentlemen did, but Drew stopped. He met this other one, not a lady, I'm sure. A highflier though. Lydia Denham was her name—a blackhaired, scheming jade. She was that quiet about her connection with Drew. Then there was this masquerade at Lady Somebody-or-other's, a regular high stickler, and this Lydia got Drew to take her.

"Meanwhile Cyril had cut out all the others with Miss Chilton, and there was an announcement in the *Gazette*, and the earl handed out extra horns of ale for everybody. So it seemed everything was all right and tight. But you see this masquerade brought them all together." Ned was warming up to his story now. "So this Lydia, bold as brass, takes off her mask smack in front of the beauty and Cy and introduces herself as his lordship's last fancy piece. Then she says—" Here Ned altered his voice. " 'It is a pity you have not been able to compare the two brothers as I have, Miss Chilton; you might have chosen differently.' "

Margaret stared at him, trying to comprehend the effect of such a public moment of humiliation on a proud, cold spirit like the viscount's.

"It was in all the print shops," Ned said solemnly. "And Miss Chilton sent a notice to the papers that she and the viscount wouldn't suit after all."

"Cyril must have taken some revenge," Margaret prompted.

"I think he did, but no one knows really, except Cy and Drew. I know Cy bought up Drew's vowels and bills. Lydia choused Drew out of a pretty penny, you may be sure. Then the old earl called Drew down to Haddon, not straightaway though. Didn't shout or rage at him at all, just icy cold, and Drew went to Humphrey. The old man called all the household together and told us Drew was not his son anymore and no one was to speak to him or help him in any way and we were to report him as a trespasser if he showed his face on Haddon land."

Margaret was puzzled. She considered what she had heard in the brothel. "So the earl did not disown him immediately?" she asked, certain that somehow there was more to it.

"No," said Ned, "that's the strange part. It was about a month later. The prattle-boxes in the kitchen were talking about other gossip already."

"But everyone thought the earl disowned him over the scrape with Miss Denham?"

"Yes, what else?"

Margaret sighed. "I think there must be something else, but now you must tell me what happened after he was disowned and how he knew that Cyril was going to steal the papers."

"Well, he gave up women, said as he had neither love nor money to give 'em, he wouldn't be taking anything either." Ned shook his head doubtfully.

"Is there something surprising in that, Ned?" Margaret asked. "I should think he would very much dislike my sex after Miss Denham's betrayal and the trouble she caused him." She thought it no wonder he had not wished to see her again.

"Oh, aye, miss, but it's not that easy to say no to a skirt."

Margaret wanted to press him for further explanation, but she knew she must get to the heart of Drew's present danger. She looked at Ned, encouraging him to go on.

"Well, this part I know. A fellow in the War Office told Drew—because whatever the rest of the quality thought, the swells in the War Office aren't easily taken in—anyway, this fellow told Drew that recent leaks had been traced to the earl. It seems that Hookey divides up his information, sends a bit to one fellow, some other bit to someone else, and never tells the whole of it to anyone, and the bits that were getting to the Frenchies were coming from the earl. So Drew figured out the rest, and you know what happened after that," Ned finished. He stood and stretched and said he must be going.

"Going?" said Margaret. "But we haven't made our plan to save him yet."

Ned groaned. He opened his mouth to protest, and Margaret opened hers to forestall him.

"I know," he said ruefully, "if we don't do something, he'll die."

Margaret smiled appreciatively at this sign of understanding. "Do you think he could be persuaded to leave London?"

"Now? No. Where do you think he would go?"

"To America, to make a new life," Margaret offered.

"Even if you could persuade him, and I don't think you could, he has none of the ready," said Ned dampeningly.

Margaret loosened the strings of her reticule and drew forth the sapphires and the ring. "We could sell these, Ned," she suggested, "and he would have a grand sum."

Ned stared at the glittering jewels. "You must be dicked in the nob—begging your pardon, miss, but we couldn't sell those without somebody saying we stole 'em. Besides, he wouldn't want 'em sold. He gave them to you?"

"Yes, that first night, in Humphrey's cottage." She had a sudden recollection of that very strange moment when Drew had fastened the sapphires around her neck and she had first seen herself as someone else.

"Then he must be in a bad way about you, miss. Those were his mother's."

"His mother's?" She was stunned, remembering what she had thought about him at the time. How wrong she had been from the beginning.

"Aye. Didn't you see the big painting of her in the hall?"

"I suppose I paid no attention, but the necklace can't mean that he loves me. He gave it to me before we ever . . ." Her voice trailed away. "If he loves me, why would he want me to marry someone else?"

"You think a man's going to ask a woman to share his disgrace? I didn't think so, miss, but maybe you've got more hair than wit." Ned really did make to leave then, and the fear of it made Margaret quick. She

leaped to her feet and scurried around in front of him
to block his path.

"Ned," she began warningly. "We have to get
Drew out of disgrace to save him. We have to convince the earl that he was wrong to disown Drew,
and I know he'd be convinced if only he had heard
them in that brothel."

"Convince the earl he was wrong!" Ned scorned
the proposal as he would have scorned a suggestion
that they fly. "The quality don't admit to being wrong
much, miss," he said. "Besides, we don't know what
really happened to make the old man do it, so we
don't know what we have to prove." He halted, a
little bewildered by his own logic.

But Margaret was suddenly inspired. "You are
right, Ned. We don't know. Only Cyril and Drew
know. They are the only ones who can convince the
earl, so we must get them to do it." Ned looked at
her as if she were quite mad. "We need to bring them
together where the earl can overhear them. It's like
a play, Ned. Like *Lear*, or *Othello*, or *Hamlet*."

"I don't know who any of those fellows are, miss.
Swells, to be sure, but I don't think they know the
earl or Cy."

"No, of course not, Ned, for they are all characters
in Shakespeare's plays. Cy and Drew are the characters in our play, and the earl, of course."

"Our play?" said Ned, looking quite baffled.

"Yes, Ned," said Margaret firmly. "You and I are
going to write a play. *Truth Triumphs* or some such
nonsense, and we're going to set it in ... in Vauxhall," she finished. "Meet me here tomorrow morning, as soon as you are able, and I'll tell you your
part." She gathered up the remains of Ned's food and
drink and pulled her cloak about her, preparing to
dash to the house.

It was still raining, and Ned wished he hadn't lost
his hat. He turned up his collar.

"What am I going to say to Drew tonight?" he asked.

"Lie," said Margaret, smiling a brilliant smile at him. Then she was gone.

"Lord," said Ned, and stepped out into the rain.

16

THOSE OF THE *ton* who remarked Margaret Somerley's vivacity at Lady Nevin's ball attributed it to
various causes. There were young ladies who believed it quite selfish and perhaps wicked of Margaret
to attract so many partners, and there were matrons
of Lady Somerley's years who were inclined to believe
Margaret's dress had wrought the change. It was of
a yellow sarsanet so pale it might have been distilled
sunlight. The bodice was simplicity itself, gathered
into a darker yellow cord, threaded like a garland
across her white shoulders, and the layers of dainty
pin tucks at the hem, ornamented with a single white
rose, lent the whole quite a note of elegance.

The young men who found themselves vying for
the lady's favor could scarcely have said why. Miss
Somerley seemed to be so interested in whatever a
fellow had to say. It was the easiest thing in the world
to talk to her about one's horses or guns or military
tactics or mills or how the fireworks at Vauxhall were
accomplished. She listened attentively and asked just
the sort of questions that allowed one to say more
about one's favorite topic. Still the young man who
attempted to explain all this to Viscount Lyndhurst
could not help but feel uneasy at his lordship's deep-

ening frown. Perhaps the wags at the clubs, who were saying that Cyril Durant meant to fix his interest with the girl, were right.

Margaret did not realize that she had made a tactical error in appearing so lively until the viscount, with calculated charm, invited her driving. Even then she would have refused him had he not extended the invitation in the presence of Lady Somerley. Before her mother Margaret could not refuse an invitation from a man to whom, in her parents' eyes, she owed so great a debt. His insistence that they drive at an unfashionably early hour confirmed her fear that his suspicions were aroused. Blindly she danced two more sets, and the young men, who had counted themselves fortunate to have secured her as a partner, were left to wonder at the sudden change in her manner. The girl had wilted faster than a man's shirt points in a hot ballroom. Lady Somerley, alarmed at the sudden listlessness of her daughter and concerned that Margaret be in her best looks for what promised to be a significant morning interview, sent for the Somerley carriage.

A faint mist was rising from the rain-soaked roofs and pavement when Margaret left the cold stables. Ned had not appeared. Reluctantly she returned to the house. She could not afford to annoy or upset her parents should the viscount arrive and she be found missing. Everything had gone as she wished until Cyril Durant had maneuvered her into driving with him. Her parents had been only too pleased to organize a party for the gardens. Her mother had supplied the names of a dozen or more guests they ought to include. Her father had readily agreed to the renting of a large supper box. In the interval between her meeting with Ned and their departure for the Nevins' ball Margaret had searched her father's volume of Shakespeare's plays, looking for those scenes of eavesdropping that might suggest to her how she was to assemble her own cast of characters at Vauxhall.

She knew very well that a message to the earl that he would hear of his missing papers at Vauxhall would bring that gentleman, and she had no doubt Cyril would come to the appointed place for the information she offered him. She believed she had assigned Ned a role even he could perform without confusion, and she had provided for him a domino of her father's. Only her message to Drew had taxed her invention. It was one thing to tell Ned to lie to him and quite another to do so herself. In the end she had settled for a direct appeal.

Dear Drew, she had written, blushing as if he were there to hear her first use of the intimate address.

Please come to me at Vauxhall. Ned will explain when and where. Signing this brief epistle occasioned further agonies of indecision, but at last she simply wrote *Meg* as that was what she most wished to hear.

These were the messages she must now entrust to Betsy to deliver into Ned's hands, if indeed Ned meant to keep their appointment.

Cyril Durant's curricle with its bottle-green trim was a sleek, shining equipage, as elegant as the man himself, the tiny tiger as proudly liveried as one of the prince's own. Margaret suspected that in all of London there could not be a female more reluctant to enter it than she was. But she accepted the viscount's hand and seated herself with as much assurance as she could command. She would not, however, speak first. She contrived to look about her as if she had nothing to fear and could truly enjoy the freshness of the morning.

Thus, as they passed through the northwest corner of Grosvenor Square, she received a painful shock. A man of enormous proportions was being assisted into a black traveling chaise. The dangerous tilt of the vehicle as the man's weight rested upon the steps immediately recalled to Margaret's mind the last time she had seen Croisset enter his carriage.

The realization of all that the Frenchman's presence in London must mean deprived her of further awareness of her surroundings. The viscount had turned his curricle into the park and had instructed his tiger to jump down before she recovered in some measure from the apprehension that had seized her at the sight of Croisset. One adversary must not make her weak in the face of another.

"Miss Somerley, do not think to fool me as you have the *ton*," the viscount began, directing a penetrating stare at her. He set the horses into easy motion through the nearly deserted park. "Your remarkable vivacity last night can only mean you have met with my brother."

"But I have not, my lord," said Margaret, with just enough presence of mind to speak calmly. "I have neither seen him nor heard from him."

"Then perhaps, my dear, your happiness last night was the happiness of anticipation," he suggested. This was harder to deny, and it required great strength of will for Margaret to meet his gaze.

"Ah, of course," said the viscount. "The Vauxhall gardens scheme. Your mother mentioned it to me last night. An ideal spot for a lovers' tryst."

Margaret looked away. If he thought that, he might still accompany them to the gardens in the hope of catching Drew, but not if he guessed her true purpose. What would he think when he received the note she had sent through Ned?

"Perhaps," her companion continued, "more than a tryst. Perhaps an elopement?"

Margaret turned to him in amazement. "Your brother, my lord, will keep his word to you. He will not run away from the game."

"But you have made me no such assurances, have

you, Miss Somerley? You would run away and leave me to be shot by the French, would you not?" He flicked the reins, sending the horses into a brisk, jarring trot.

There could be no conversation at this pace, and Margaret found herself curiously unsettled. She must tell him she had seen Croisset. She could not in conscience conceal his danger. But she thought the bitterness of the man beside her would destroy him even if Croisset did not. As soon as the carriage slowed, she spoke.

"I do not wish you to be shot, my lord," she said, but he only laughed.

"Then you must name a gentleman whose attentions you particularly wish to encourage."

"There is no such gentleman, as you well know," Margaret confessed.

"Think, Miss Somerley. Nearly all your mother's hopes for you are realized. Is she to be disappointed when her expectations are highest?" he asked.

It would be of no use to plead the unfairness of his tactics, for Margaret understood too well that she must choose between Drew and her parents. She remained silent, wondering if anything she could say would heal the breach between the brothers.

"You will not name the man?" the viscount continued in his indifferent way. "Alas, I can wait no longer."

"So you have not been able to find him," said Margaret. Her plan might succeed after all, in spite of her adversary's suspicions.

Then, as if he had read her thoughts, he said, "I, too, have plans. It seems I cannot rely on the greed of my fellow Londoners to deliver him into my hands, so I must lure him out of whatever unholy sanctuary he has found."

They had nearly completed their circuit of the park,

moving again at the languid pace that characterized the viscount at his most controlled.

"An announcement of our engagement in tomorrow's *Gazette*, which can be corrected later when we decide we do not suit, should suffice to bring my brother out of hiding."

"He won't believe it, my lord," Margaret ventured, trying to conceal her alarm at the deception he proposed.

"Miss Somerley, you underestimate the rage a man feels to think of his love in the arms of another. The barest possibility that I might have you in my bed will make my brother quite reckless." The tone of this speech was much stronger than any she had heard from him before, and she was reminded of the scandal that had ended his engagement. His mistress had played him false and taunted him with it publicly. His betrothed had deserted him.

They had reached the entrance to the park. Margaret must tell him about Croisset, but if she did, would he not publish the announcement of their engagement as he threatened and would it not bring Drew out of hiding at the very time of greatest danger? Her conscience would not be denied, yet she scarcely knew how to begin.

"I do not wish you ill, my lord," she said, knowing how little likely he was to believe her, thinking she must, nevertheless, win some measure of trust from him.

"Yet you wish my brother well?" She nodded. "It cannot be, my dear. One cannot wish both sides well in a duel, a battle." He spoke as if he regretted his enmity toward his brother, and Margaret allowed herself a measure of hope.

"Yes, one can," she urged, "for one can wish for peace, for brothers to be reconciled." In her eagerness to be believed, she reached out and touched his arm. A look she could only describe as hungry crossed his

face fleetingly. But when he spoke, his words were
those she had ever heard from him.

"How well-suited you and my noble brother are,"
he mocked, "dreamers both. Do you know how much
satisfaction it gives me to keep you apart? To watch
you pine for him, to imagine his misery at having
given you up? And the ultimate satisfaction, to taunt
him with the prospect of you in another man's bed—
do you think I could give that up?"

"I don't believe you," said Margaret, trembling.
She had to deny his words, as much for his sake as
for hers. It was too painful to look on this man, in
face and form so like her love, yet consumed with
hatred. "I think you wish to love your brother," she
dared to say, though she could not be sure he heard
her.

They had reached North Audley Street, and the
moment for honest speech was at hand, yet Margaret
feared to speak for she had only stirred the viscount's
temper with her efforts to prepare him for her revelation.

"My lord," she said, summoning her courage, "you
must know—Croisset is in London."

His hands on the reins gave a little jerk, so that the
horses sidestepped abruptly, startling a passing
gentleman, who frowned fiercely at the viscount.

"What's this, Miss Somerley?" her companion
asked, recovering his ease of manner. "A little piece
of the truth? Why so forthcoming now?" he continued, his voice cold. "Is it a desire to taunt the condemned man? Or is it that having made your plans
for escape with your lover, your conscience pricks you
at my fate?"

"Please, my lord," Margaret pleaded, "you must
believe me sincere. You and Drew could stop Croisset. I know Drew would be willing to put aside the
past if you would join him now. He did suggest it,
you know, that night in the brothel." Too late she

understood how her words confirmed his suspicion that she had met with his brother.

Though he didn't speak, she sensed the terrible rage in him. They had reached her parents' door, but instead of reining in, the viscount unexpectedly cracked his whip so that the horses bolted. Margaret clutched the side of the vehicle.

The particular peril of careening down the streets of Mayfair, where at any turn they might run someone down or collide with another carriage, passed soon enough. The viscount brought his startled and no longer fresh team under control, and Margaret did not venture to say anything lest she enrage him further. Still he did not turn back toward the fashionable quarter of London as she hoped, but toward the city. Nor did he speak until they entered narrower, busier streets.

As before when Drew had brought her into the town from the docks, Margaret lost her bearings. One minute they had been passing down a wide thoroughfare of respectable shops amid the cheerful bustle of prosperous Londoners doing business, the next they had entered a dim and noisome street, where the press and jostle of the crowd was no less energetic but decidedly sinister.

"Do you recall the neighborhood, Miss Somerley?" the viscount asked. "Is there someone on whom you would wish to make a morning call? May I drop you somewhere?"

Margaret met his taunting gaze directly. Here their carriage and clothes seemed to draw greedy and calculating stares from every side. She felt the strings of her reticule give and the little bag slip from her arm, but, turning, she could not see anyone near who could have taken it from her. A miserable young woman with a babe in arms, a crippled man bent over his cane, vendors with wares in hand crying out to win a purchase from their fellows. In all there was an air of desperate striving, of predatory alertness. It was to these very streets that the most practiced thieves of London retreated with their booty, and the law, such as it was, did not follow. Grimly she waited for the viscount's rage to cool and his rational powers to reassert themselves.

Just when she thought them hopelessly lost, a turn or two, no more, brought them to a shabby but less menacing district, where the energies of the populace seemed to find their outlet in honest labor. Two young men were painting the bright trim of a shop front; a row of costermongers' stalls appeared to attract as many honest buyers as thieves; a drayman's cart piled with grain sacks stood ready to be unloaded at the sign of a public house. Margaret looked down and found she had made tight fists of her mittened hands. She uncurled her fingers and smoothed the folds of her skirt, but she could not calm her mind as easily. Thus occupied, she did not see the arrested expression on the face of the young man at the back of the drayman's cart.

He was a strong fellow for all his fair looks and threadbare corduroys. If the girl did not see him stare, his companion did and gave him a friendly elbow in the ribs. "That one's never for you, my lad, for all your golden looks." When the younger man continued to gaze after the girl in the passing carriage as if he had been struck deaf and dumb, the older man spoke crossly. "Pick it up, man. Best be looking to Molly inside for what you want, she'll give it to you right enough." The shining vehicle disappeared around a corner. Only then did the young man heft one of the weighty sacks onto his shoulder and turn from the street.

At Margaret's door, the viscount left his curricle in the care of his tiger, who was waiting for them on the steps. Her companion coldly insisted on accompanying her inside. "Your mother will have callers," he warned quietly as she looked to flee up the stairs. As the butler opened the doors to the yellow salon, Margaret endeavored to compose her face at least, for she feared she must give a very singular appearance if her looks reflected any of her agitation. Even in her shocked and unhappy state it was clear to her how her entrance on the viscount's arm would lend credence to rumors of an attachment between them.

He hardly seemed to notice and led Margaret to a seat with his customary cool civility. "I must speak with your mother about these plans of hers for a Vauxhall entertainment," he whispered. "I hardly think it is quite the thing for you to go tomorrow. Too large an element of the vulgar present, who may be inclined to offer insult to a young woman like yourself." Powerless to protest among her mother's acquaintance, Margaret glared at him. So this was to be his revenge. How had she dreamed that she could reach the better part of his nature?

She had reasoned and pleaded in vain. Futilely, she had reminded her mother of all that Lady Somerley had told her of the wonders of Vauxhall—of the fireworks, dancing, and cascade, and the romantic corner where her parents had once dined tête-à-tête under bright lanterns among great Corinthian columns—all that had been promised Margaret in her turn. In the end, wearied beyond thought, she had refused supper and declined to accompany her parents to the theatre. They would be ruled by the fashionable Cyril Durant, and all Margaret's plans would come to nothing. The earl and Drew would stumble around in the dark and wonder at the urgent notes each had received. The dreadful announcement of her betrothal would appear in the papers, and Drew would fall into the viscount's hands to be offered to the French. She could think no further about what must inevitably follow. She was quite blind with the sting of it in her eyes and paralyzed with the ache of it in her heart. There could be no greater misery.

Yet her first thought the following morning was that things might indeed be worse. Cyril Durant might connect the note she had sent him with his suspicions of her plans. Purporting to be an anonymous informant, she had promised the viscount news about his brother if he would meet the black domino at Vauxhall. Cyril would not need to publish an announcement in the papers. He could lay a trap for Drew at Vauxhall, and Drew would go to his death imagining that she had betrayed him, for hadn't she pleaded that he meet her at the gardens. It was an appointment she must keep.

Impatiently she waited, praying for Ned to appear at his corner, and when he did, she chafed under the tedious delay of donning her pelisse, bonnet, and gloves. She barely concealed her haste in collecting Betsy and excusing herself to her mother. As they passed his corner, she whispered her message to Ned and then all but ran to the park and back. Only once did she slacken her pace—at the sight of Croisset's black traveling chaise slowly circling Grosvenor Square. What did it mean? How close was Croisset to acting against the viscount?

In the stable she fairly flung herself into Ned's arms.

"Here now, miss," he protested, holding her at arm's length. "What's happened to overset you?"

"Did you deliver my messages?" she cried.

"Every one," he assured her.

"Oh, Ned," she exclaimed, "my parents have canceled our party to Vauxhall." She poured out her fears, ending with the greatest, the ever-present threat that Drew would die. "So you must take me, Ned, for I must get to Vauxhall tonight."

"It's a bird-witted idea, Miss," said Ned, "to go without your mama and papa. How are we to get there? Did you think I could bring round my coach and four?"

"We'll go by hack and scull. I've brought the money for the hack with me, so you can hire one and meet me at your corner." She fished in her reticule for the coins. "Admission is only a shilling, and I've got that, too."

"And how are you to get out the door of your papa's fine house, miss? And suppose someone sees you there that knows you, even Cy?"

"I shall contrive, Ned, and I mean to wear a domino, too, so no one will remark my appearance at all."

"I don't like it," said Ned flatly. "I should go and warn Drew off, and you should stay home, right and tight in your bed."

"But Ned, together we will have two pairs of eyes and ears with which to find him, and I could never bear to wait till morning not knowing if he lives or dies." It was unfair, but Margaret had learned that she need only mention the possibility of Drew's dying to win Ned over to any plan. "You don't have a pistol, do you, Ned?"

"Lord," said Ned.

17

DREW STOOD IN the shadowed alleyway, observing the entrance to the gardens. It had been at Vauxhall that he had met Lydia Denham, he reflected. In retrospect, of course, he realized that their meeting had been carefully contrived by the lady. What he had believed a chance encounter had been part of her scheme of revenge. How well she had picked her instrument, for nothing could have wounded Cy more than yet another comparison to himself. Of course, it had been no part of Lydia's scheme that he be disinherited or disgraced, but he doubted that the events had caused her any regret. And he could not blame her for his own impulsive nature that had allowed him to be played upon as he had been.

Here he was again, yielding to yet another impulse. He should not allow himself to see Meg tonight, and he would not if she had not used his name in her note and if he had not seen her only the day before in Lions Lane where he should have been safe from temptation. She had been looking down, smoothing her skirt, and in his mind's eye he had seen that little gesture of feminine dignity a thousand times since. Every instinct he had sharpened in play and war told him he was walking into danger, yet he paid his shilling and entered the gardens.

He drifted in and out among the crowds, never straying far from the entrance. He might be in rags, but his appearance was hardly remarked in the midst of dominos and more ambitious forms of masquerade. The crowd had such an air of gaiety, that if he did not know better, he would have supposed even the thieves and Cyprians to be on holiday. At last his vigilance was rewarded for he saw his brother enter, escorting a diminutive lady in a black domino.

The lady in the domino was like Meg in size, but he could not see her face or hair. Whatever plan Meg had made to meet him, he was sure it did not include her coming to the gardens with only his brother as escort. Still the lady in the domino could be Meg. He remembered well Cy's threat to act against her, and he had seen Cy's rage and Meg's fear as they passed him in Lions Lane. So Drew followed them as they made their way around the main grove, past the dancers under the great kiosk, and up one of the colonnaded walks through the third arch, just as Ned had described it to him. The bell for the fireworks rang.

He continued to follow them up a smaller path, lit dimly at intervals by the colored lanterns for which Vauxhall was known. And he turned as they did into a grove and approached a small replica of a ruined temple with its steps leading to a dais and its columns festooned with strings of lanterns. He felt for the pistol in his coat pocket. Cyril was gone. The lady in the domino stood alone in the center of the dais, her manner shrinking and uncertain. He remembered how Meg had trembled in his arms at seeing the Viper. Because the girl on the dais could be Meg, he must go to her.

"Ned," whispered Margaret, removing her mask and pushing back the hood of her mother's lavender domino, "whatever *I* do or say, *you* must stay concealed until the last possible moment." They had reached the gardens in time to hear the bell for the fireworks, and it had been easy enough with her mother's remembrances fresh in her ears to find the little path to the grove of the temple. They had seen no one come the same way, but Margaret could not risk any further speech, for she did not know who of her cast had already assembled in the mild darkness. Ned mumbled something about harebrained and bird-witted notions, but he subsided as they moved cautiously forward through the trees.

Drew stepped out of the shadows into the lantern light and called softly to the silent figure on the dais, "Meg?" The girl turned to his voice, lifting her face. As like Meg as she was in stature and figure, her face was startlingly different—thin and pale, framed with black hair, and made catlike with green, glowing eyes. Drew whirled, but Cyril was already there, pistol leveled.

"Run along, my dear," he said to the frightened young Cyprian. "You have played your part admirably." With his free hand he offered the girl some coins that clinked solidly in her palm. His gaze never left Drew. "Come, brother," he said, "we must have you take the stage in this little drama your love has arranged."

"Where is Meg?" Drew asked, backing up the steps to the low platform.

"Meg, is it?" mocked Cyril. "You do have the common touch, don't you, brother. She's betrayed you. She quite enjoys her success, you know. In the clubs they're saying she might catch herself a viscount."

"Betrayal is not in her nature, Cy. What have you done with her?" Drew tried to quell a sick feeling in the pit of his stomach that his brother might have

harmed her. Perhaps he ought not to have counted
on Cy's rationality and fastidiousness.

"What a touching faith you have in women,
brother," Cyril continued. "I've done nothing with
her, of course. I merely suggested to Lord and Lady
Somerley that I could not quite like their Vauxhall
scheme. Too free and easy a crowd for my taste. I
imagine Miss Somerley is spending the evening in
her chamber, most distraught over your impending
demise."

Drew almost laughed. "You relieve my mind, Cy.
I take it Meg has not accepted an offer of marriage
yet and you have grown impatient with the delay?"

There was a moment of silence. "But you knew that
when you came here tonight," said Cyril in a puzzled
tone. "Indeed, you must know the girl will hardly
promise herself to another while you live, and so, you
see, you have not played fairly with me, brother, and
you cannot blame me if I now play to win."

The only sounds in the little grove were the faint
tinkle of distant music and from somewhere a burst
of brittle laughter. To Margaret, coming upon the
scene at this moment, the two men might have been
stone—Cyril, a lean figure of elegant malice; Drew,
marble unconcern—the composition held in place by
the glinting steel in Cyril's hand.

"Am I about to die then, Cy?" Drew asked.

As imperfectly as she understood what had passed
before on the dais, this Margaret understood. "No!"
she shouted. It was a cry of the heart, and both men
turned toward the sound, the viscount stepping back
a little, brandishing his pistol against any sudden
move the younger man might make. Margaret started
forward in her pale, shimmering domino, stumbling
a little in her haste.

"Stay in the shadows, Meg," Drew called, but it
was too late.

She caught up her skirts and took the steps to the

little platform. It was indeed like a stage, at the edge of which she stopped, held back by the viscount's gleaming pistol. She would have to pass him to reach Drew.

"Well, Miss Somerley," said the viscount, "how determined you are to keep your appointments. I see I quite underestimated you, but I am afraid the elopement is off."

"My lord," said Margaret, "there was never to be an elopement." She paused to catch her breath. "But there must be an end to this mad game you are playing, and the truth must be told." This last she addressed to Drew, looking at him directly, but his gaze scanned the darkness beyond her, and he seemed intent on the cry of bird.

"Oh, I mean to end the game, here and now," the viscount assured her. He raised his pistol arm a fraction of an inch higher. "My brother, you see, is about to be wounded . . . by footpads, I think. Because he is out of favor with my father, I will have him conveyed to my own quarters where he will receive the best medical care." He paused. "Of course, it will be a terrible shock when a second, successful attempt on his life is made."

"Why do you tell me this, my lord?" Margaret asked. "Do you think I can witness such acts and remain silent? Do you think me powerless to stop you?" She lunged forward. If she could do nothing else, she meant to throw her body in front of Drew's, but the viscount caught the hood of her domino and yanked her back, nearly choking her. He pressed his pistol sharply into her side and secured a hold on her with his other arm about her shoulders.

Drew had moved too, springing forward to meet her, but unable to cover the distance in time. "Damn you, Cy," he swore. "Let her go. You have me." But Cyril shook his head and jabbed the pistol in Margaret's ribs, emphasizing his command of the situation. Again Margaret saw Drew's quick glance at the trees.

"Interesting," came another voice from the darkness. There was a rustling of leaves, and then an enormous man in black stepped forward. Like Cyril Durant he held a pistol. He was accompanied by two men of quite ordinary proportions similarly armed. At a quick order in French these moved to flank their master.

"So this is how it was done, how Croisset was tricked," the fat man mused aloud. "I had not known there were brothers." He lumbered closer to them so that Margaret could see the black pinpoints of his eyes in the white, bloated face. For a long moment he said nothing but stared closely at the two men on the dais. "So one is a hero, the English patriot who tries to make a fool out of Croisset and the Viper, and one is the spy who steals the father's papers. But which is which?"

No one spoke. Through the layers of thin silk and taffeta she wore Margaret could feel the circle of steel pressed against her side, concealed from Croisset's view by the folds of her domino.

"Croisset," began the viscount, "my brother here is the man you want. Your fortuitous arrival saves me the trouble of bringing him to you."

The fat man did not answer for some time. "So you say," he at last replied. "But the man who met me at Highcliffe was an elegant gentleman, like yourself, and like yourself he had his arms about this girl. Oh, yes, I remember well." Margaret stood perfectly still, amazed at the irony that Cyril's threat to her now endangered his life.

"Perhaps," said Cyril, "the gentleman you met merely impersonated me, and the girl is no more than a scheming whore who has played us both false."

"Perhaps," said the Frenchman, with a shrug that

rippled down his huge frame. "I would like to hear the other gentleman speak."

"What would you have me say, Croisset?" asked Drew coolly. "Would you like a third possibility? Perhaps you have been deceived not by one man, but by two, working together. Perhaps you have walked into a trap."

A fierce silence followed this suggestion, the Frenchman's displeasure apparent not in words but in the hostile concentration of his gaze, as if he could burn away the disguises of those before him. Then he smiled with awful satisfaction, and that common expression of goodwill further distorted his unpleasant face.

"I will play Solomon," he announced. "You," he addressed Cyril, pointing his gun, "release the girl." Margaret felt Cyril's hold loosen, felt the press of the gun against her ribs disappear and Cyril's hand drop subtly to his side. "You," Croisset commanded her, "move to the center." Cautiously she stepped away from the viscount. "More," said Croisset. She took another step. She dared not look at Drew lest she betray him as the man the French wanted. Should she call on Ned, or would such action only alert Croisset? Was the earl out there somewhere in the darkness? In the distance the fireworks began, pops and booms and bursts of delighted applause from the crowd.

Croisset seemed to listen for a moment. "Good," he said. He pointed the pistol directly at Margaret and advanced a couple of ponderous steps in her direction. "I will count to ten," he said, "as we do for the duel, gentlemen. At ten, I shoot the girl. This man I want, he loves the girl, he will step in front of her before I fire. It is your English way, is it not? So, I shoot him. My honor is restored. The Viper's honor is restored." He began to count.

"Stop!"

The brusque command, ringing out from the darkness behind Croisset, had, ironically, the opposite effect on all the actors of the little drama. Croisset jerked, turning his head toward the new voice. Too large for swift action, he staggered heavily, struggling to maintain his balance, his pistol firing wide of its mark. Cyril, who shifted his aim to meet the new threat, gasped as the other's bullet hit him before he could fire.

Even as the stranger's cry diverted his enemies, Drew sprang for Margaret and pulled her behind him. "Ned," he yelled before she had time to think it. He slipped the pistol free of his pocket and returned Croisset's fire, hitting the Frenchman in the neck. A second shot from the man in the trees brought Croisset down. The felled spy's two henchmen crouched low, guns still aimed at the brothers when Ned came hurtling out of the dark, knocking down the man standing behind Cyril. For an instant the two brothers faced each other across the dais. Drew's weapon hung at his side. His other arm held Margaret behind him. Cyril smiled faintly, steadied the gun pointed at his brother, and fired. There was a sharp cry from Croisset's second accomplice behind Drew, who crumpled to the ground an instant before the viscount himself collapsed.

Drew released Margaret and rushed to his brother's side. "Where did Croisset hit you, Cy?" he asked, kneeling and attempting to pull away the viscount's intricate cravat. Cyril's hand on his stopped him.

"It's no use to inquire," Cyril said in a faint, breathless voice. His eyes closed momentarily, and Margaret, kneeling also, took his other hand in hers. It was icy cold.

"I owe you my life, Cy," Drew whispered.

"No," said Cyril, opening his eyes again. "I just missed. Never was as good a shot as you were . . .

Drew." The hand holding Drew's tightened momentarily, then went slack.

"Get away from my son," came a gruff voice. Then the earl stood over them, pistol in hand, glaring down as if with his gaze he could annihilate them. Margaret rose and stepped back a step. Drew stood more slowly, facing his father.

"Is there no end to the pain and disgrace you would bring upon your house, sir?" the earl asked. Margaret saw Drew flinch at his father's words. "Get out of my sight."

"No," Margaret cried, reaching out to him, but he had begun to back away. He looked up once from the foot of the dais, all the blue lights in his eyes quite out.

"Good-bye, Meg," he said softly. Then in two strides he disappeared among the trees. She started to run after him, but Ned caught her and stopped her.

"You won't catch him tonight, miss."

"Drew," she called helplessly, her cry lost amid the deserted groves of the least pleasurable garden she had ever entered.

18

I T RAINED THE day Cyril Durant, Viscount Lyndhurst, was buried. The drizzle that dampened
mourners and spectators alike perhaps restrained the
curiosity of those who had come from London merely
on the chance they might glean some tidbit of gossip
about the lofty viscount. Margaret did not overhear
anything like the rumors of the past two days in town.
There the *on-dit* was that the viscount had been involved in some shocking intrigue with French spies.
Nor was she conscious of more than an occasional
interested stare in her direction as she stood beside
her parents in the church and later at the grave.

She had insisted on making the journey to Haddon,
though her parents had been willing to excuse her
from any obligation to the dead man and his family.
Her explanation and confession had seen to that. In
those first hours after she and Ned had returned to
North Audley Street, she had laid the most complete
set of facts before her father. She had endured his
disappointment over her own role in events and his
indignation over the actions of the Durant brothers.
And she had risked his anger in her defense of Ned
and of Drew. Later she had been obliged to give less
detailed accounts to her mother and several gentle-

men with legal and military authority. Still, in nearly three days of talk about the circumstances leading to the viscount's death, she had not spoken to the one whose forgiveness and understanding she most wanted to have, the Earl of Haddon.

Since that night in the gardens he had had a stark, withered look. With his height, his shock of white hair, his mourning clothes, he now looked like nothing so much as a tree blasted by lightning. Every movement, every expression spoke pain, and his desolation both frightened Margaret and stirred her compassion.

Her message about the stolen papers had brought him to the gardens, armed and with a rear guard of gentlemen from the War Office. She wished she could beg his pardon for her disastrous plan, and she wished she could tell him of the nobility of *both* of his sons in those terrible moments at Vauxhall. But she could not intrude on his grief while it was so new, so raw. So she resolved to stay at Haddon as long as she could, waiting for that moment when the earl would wonder how he had come to lose both of his sons at one stroke. She hoped the moment would come soon enough to save Drew Durant.

The moment came, as such moments can, almost without warning. Margaret had claimed the library as her refuge during this, her third and most unhappy visit to Haddon. Each evening she returned to the cream silk wing chair in which she had been sitting the night Drew Durant had stepped through the open window into her life. She had been free to retreat in this manner because Lady Somerley had returned to Wynrose following the viscount's funeral. The baronness' nerves had not been equal to the strain of the earl's grief, Margaret's stubbornness, and Baron Somerley's preoccupation with helping his friend settle the viscount's affairs. Thus Margaret was alone in the library when the earl entered with a gentleman she recognized as someone from the War Office.

She rose at once and curtsied, murmuring her excuses. But the visiting gentleman crossed the room and took her hand.

"Miss Somerley, good evening," he said. "I must thank you again for your willingness to answer so many of our questions in this dreadful affair. I think you will be happy to know we have traced a number of Croisset's contacts along the coast. His network will no longer send information to the French." He patted her hand in an avuncular way and released it. Margaret turned to go but did not get out the door before she heard the earl's visitor whisper, "A brave one, that girl."

The earl's summons came within the hour. A footman ushered Margaret into the library and deserted her before she had taken two steps into the room, two steps which did not begin to cover the distance between her and the earl. To reach him she must take a dozen more steps under his fierce scrutiny. He offered no word of encouragement, but Margaret, thinking of all that he had lost and that which she hoped she might help him regain, advanced.

She took the seat to which he gestured and waited as he paced before her. In his movements she saw the quick energies of one son. In his cold features, the pride of the other. When he spoke, however, he surprised her with words and tone far from those his fierce expression had led her to expect.

"Was I wrong about him, Miss Somerley?" he asked, coming to a halt in front of her. For all the abruptness of his question, the tormenting doubt in it was plain. She had no need to ask to whom he referred.

"*I* was wrong about him, my lord," she began, wishing to acknowledge her own errors before presuming to comment on his. "I thought him a thief and a traitor." Her words seemed to transfix her listener. His stare was no longer the unnerving one she had felt earlier; rather it was the arrested expression of one who wishes only to hear more. She went on, telling him of their beginning in the library, of Croisset and their crossing the sea, of the brothers who were waiting for them, the Douro, and the Viper, and through it all of Drew's courage and kindness. As she came to the end of her narrative, she sensed a return of his agitation. He strode away from her to the far end of the room and back again.

"You, Miss Somerley, may be excused for what you thought," he said. "You were acting on the evidence of your own eyes. But I, I who had every reason to trust my son, condemned him on hearsay and conjecture." He took another angry turn about the room, but his steps slowed noticeably as he returned. He seemed to have withdrawn to some place of misery inside himself.

"My lord," Margaret said gently, "what did happen to make you disown him?" It was a risky question to ask, and she held her breath. The earl at last sat down.

He told her the story of his discovery of important papers among Drew's personal correspondence and of a letter apparently from a French agent threatening his son with debtor's prison and worse if he did not pass along the very papers his father had discovered. The earl had then asked Cyril to investigate Drew's debts and had accepted the viscount's report that the French were holding Drew's vowels and bills.

"I was angry and disgusted over the affair with that high-flyer of his. I did not think to check the authenticity of the letter or to question how such documents came to be so handy to my notice or to doubt the motives of my oldest son. I made accusations."

"Drew did not deny them, did he?" Margaret asked. She could well imagine him at such a moment, how his eyes would change, his expression harden.

"In that he was wrong, was he not? In his pride he was at fault."

The earl did not answer. The silence between them stretched on, sad but relieved of strain by their new understanding of each other and the man they both loved. Margaret told herself to be patient; she would talk to the earl again. Perhaps she should be satisfied to have made the truth about Andrew Durant known, to have restored his father's good opinion of him. But she had hoped for much more from this conversation.

Then the earl asked, "Where is he, Miss Somerley?"

Her spirits rose at once. The earl was a man of action after all. It was not enough for him to know that he had been wrong. He must make amends.

"Oh, my lord," she said, "I do not know. He might have gone to Humphrey. He might have returned to that dreadful part of town where he was hiding before. But Ned thinks . . ."

"Ned? Ned Stow?"

"Yes, your lordship." Margaret felt the earl become distinctly wrathful at the mention of his errant groom.

"What has Ned Stow to do with my son's whereabouts?" he inquired sternly.

Margaret was obliged to explain Ned's role in Drew's bargain with Cyril and her own foolish plan. "Ned thinks," she concluded, "that Drew will join the infantry."

At this the earl jumped up. "Join the infantry? He shall not, by God. I know how to stop that. I know how to find him too, Miss Somerley. I shall do everything—hire the Runners, put out the handbills, alert the army. I shall get my son back."

"Then he is still your son?" she asked.

"He is, my dear, if he can find it in his heart to forgive me." He gave Margaret the shadow of a smile, and she gave him her assurances, said her good nights, and turned to leave.

At the door some impulse made her look back. The

earl sat at his desk with pen in hand, unseeing gaze fixed on the air. Margaret realized that she had one more truth to tell.

She and Ned had discovered the secret Cyril Durant had wished to take to his grave. It was Ned who had started her thinking in the carriage provided by the War Office as they returned from Vauxhall.

"Cy lied, miss," Ned had said.

"What do you mean?" she had asked.

"He didn't aim for Drew and miss like he said. He drilled that Frenchman clean through the heart."

As Ned spoke Margaret saw herself as she had been, kneeling at the viscount's side and holding his cold hand in hers. She saw again his other hand squeeze Drew's and in her mind heard the viscount's dying word, so faintly exhaled.

"You're right, Ned," she had said, wondering that she had not caught it at once. "Cy called him *Drew*."

At this recognition she had felt a measurable lessening of her pain, and she had resolved that should she ever see Drew Durant again she would convince him of his brother's one act of love. This little truth that the viscount had denied with his dying breath would be a great gift to give the Earl of Haddon.

"My lord," she began.

The earl's formidable energies, restored now that he had a task to do, soon produced results. Messengers and lawyers came and went at all hours; handbills appeared in the village; the household resumed its customary bustle. To Margaret's delight Ned was rescued from the position of under footman, where her father had agreed to keep him temporarily, and restored to his role in the Haddon stables. A room was prepared for the earl's only son and heir—Andrew Durant, eighth Viscount Lyndhurst. This last act unfortunately proved premature.

The days collected into weeks. The search settled

into a routine. Margaret begged her father to extend their visit and was told she might stay until her birthday, the very last day of June. She rode daily, accepting Ned's assurances that Drew would return, and read nightly, filling up the time as best she could. Once again she had found the little book of Tom True's adventures, but now it seemed to her to tell only half of the story.

The earl's missing son did not appear, and for that reason Margaret's eighteenth birthday promised to be the most dismal of her life. It rained, spoiling her ride, and the book she had depended upon to save the day failed to amuse her. But most of all, there was no news of Drew, and her bags were packed for the return to Wynrose. Thus it struck her as particularly odd that her father and the earl should be so merry whenever she chanced to pass them. At dinner their high spirits were explained. In honor of her birthday she was offered champagne and an extraordinary feast and then led blindfolded to the drawing room.

Her blindfold was removed, and she found herself facing an enormous, gaily wrapped box. There was nothing to do but accept the gentlemen's efforts with good grace and begin to unwrap. When layer after layer simply revealed another box to her, her spirits flagged a little. The experience was too like the waiting she did each day. Then she came to the last box. It had nothing in it but a folded piece of paper.

"Open it, open it," the earl urged. Both gentlemen were beaming at her with barely suppressed laughter in their eyes. She lifted the paper from the box and opened its folds. It was a document she did not at once recognize. She read the words, and blushed.

"Yes, my dear, it's a special license," said the earl. "Your father agreed I might get one for you. When my scapegrace son shows up, you may be married at once. Don't let him go."

Margaret looked from one to the other of the two men in stunned disbelief. She was to be allowed to stay. She threw her arms around her father, and then the earl must be hugged, and then they must all laugh and laugh. If only Drew would come soon.

Yet another weary interval of waiting had passed before it occurred to Margaret that it might be awkward for her to propose the use of the special license to her love, especially as she could not be sure he meant to offer for her. She sought Ned out.

She found him applying poultices to the legs of a young horse whose behavior in the traces was not what it should be.

"Ned, I have to know. Does Drew love me?" she asked.

"Lord, miss," answered her friend. He adjusted the wrappings on the animal's leg. "He loves you," he said.

"But how can you be sure?" she pressed. Margaret thought she was going to have wait for Ned to tend to each of his four-footed charges before he replied. But in the end he told her all that had transpired in the brothel after she had left, and, at her insistence, he even explained something of the difficulty her love might experience should there be a long period of betrothal. This last explanation so taxed Ned's powers of delicate speech that Margaret took pity on her friend, thanked him, and left. But the new insights she had gained from Ned's words set her thinking. Somehow she would convince her love to use the special license, for she had done quite enough waiting herself.

The open library window proved too much of a temptation. He had to look in. He told himself he would just look, for he meant to stick to his new resolves to be less impulsive, more prudent. But there she was in the great wing chair, wearing one of her white muslins, her dark, shining head bent over a book. She looked so much as she had that first evening he could not bear the delay of continuing around the terrace to the more conventional entrance to the hall. How had he let his father maneuver him into such a position? He pulled the window toward him and stepped over the low ledge.

She looked up at once. "Drew," she said, and her voice started a trembling inside him. He thought he had heard her call his name in the gardens, but he had been too stunned by his father's rejection to be sure.

"Hello, Meg," he managed. He did not move any closer.

"You have seen your father?" she asked.

"Yes," he replied, getting his voice under control. In the dim evening light he could not see her eyes as well as he wished to. He advanced a few steps in her direction.

"I'm glad," she said.

He couldn't answer; he was too occupied with taking in the sight of her, the curve of her lashes, the flush of her cheeks, a loose curl against her neck, the lace edge of her gown at her breasts. When he had gone so far in his perusal, a thought occurred that recalled him to a sense of his position. He could not be as certain of her as he wished.

Perhaps, having helped him to regain his father's trust, she felt quite free of any obligation to him. Her actions implied no particular attachment to him. Much that he had done she could complain of, much of his past might disgust her. Yet his father had made a point of mentioning her prolonged stay at Haddon.

"Meg, will you answer a question?" he asked. She nodded. "Why did you want me to meet you at Vauxhall?" Heartened by the deepening color in her cheeks as she explained her plan, he took a few more steps toward her.

"Why did you wish to see me vindicated?" he asked. Her hesitation, and the confusion in her eyes encouraged him to come closer still. But she didn't answer after all.

"If you are going to ask questions," she said, "it is only fair that I should be allowed to ask one of you." Her gaze challenged him. He nodded, and his throat felt dry. "Why have you come here tonight? I mean *here*," she emphasized, "to me."

He was still too far from her to say what he most wanted to say. A thought came to him that had quite gone out of his head the minute he had seen Meg through the window. "I came, of course, to tell you that Wellington has won a great victory at Vittoria, and that you and I may feel we contributed to his success by foiling the Viper."

"Wonderful," she said, but she stiffened, and her face appeared to lose some of the color that had suffused it a moment before. Her gaze dropped from his, and she fumbled with the book in her lap as if she did not really see it. He took advantage of her distraction and crossed the room to stand not more than inches from her. Then he reached down and lifted her chin. Her eyes were glistening with unshed tears.

"I came to ask you to marry me, Meg. Will you?" he whispered. He could see the doubt in her eyes.

"Meg," he said, "if this is your first offer and you are going to ask me if it counts, be assured that it does. Though I don't know what reasons another gentleman might have for making you an offer, I am offering for you because I love you, and I am most impatient . . ."

"Yes," she said, startling him out of any further speech.

He took the book from her hands and pulled her to her feet. He steadied her, though to have his doubts answered with such a joyful certainty left him feeling distinctly unsteady. "You know that your saying yes permits me to say and do things I could only dream of before."

"What things?" she asked. Her eyes, still bright with the glitter of unshed tears, were trusting and curious, her lips too near to resist.

"Things like this," he replied, pulling her to him and slipping his arms around her waist. "And this," he said, tightening his hold so that he felt her softness against the full length of his body. It was the first time their circumstances allowed him to savor this press of bodies, which was in itself a kiss. It was the first time his advances had not made her blush. Her clear gaze met his. Her lips parted lightly so that their breaths mingled. "And this," he whispered, touching his lips to hers.

For some time, which was inadequately measured by the earl's very modern clocks, Drew contented himself with kissing Meg. He found that the girl from whose lips he had ever had the truth was no less open and honest in this wordless language. She withheld nothing of her love, following him fearlessly into further intimacy. Her very willingness first alerted him to the danger he courted. Daring as he had always been, he had counted on Meg's resistance as a check on his own desires. But she did not stop him when he lowered his lips to her throat, and she made no protest when his trembling fingers released the tiny buttons that secured her bodice, allowing one hand to caress the softness there. The further movements he was then inspired to make at last brought him to his senses. He took hold of her upper arms and gently pushed her away from him, but he could not bring himself to let go.

Margaret watched her love closely. He had broken their embrace, but she sensed that he had done so only because they had been on the verge of some irrevocable step into passion. His grip on her arms was hard, and his breathing uneven. His coat of blue superfine stretched as smoothly as ever across his shoulders, his cravat still looked like a creditable version of a gentleman's neckwear, and his golden hair was hardly disarranged. In short he still appeared in all external ways to be the cool gentleman. But he had uncovered his heart to her, and she knew there would be no more lies between them. Now was the time to offer her thief the special license.

"I must stop, Meg," he managed. "Even our betrothal does not allow me to go on."

"But I may allow you, may I not?" she asked, recalling Ned's advice.

"You do not know the things I want to do."

But she thought she did. "I can imagine," she dared to say.

"No," he protested, and she read in the vehemence of his denial how strongly he was tempted. More calmly he said, "We must be married before I give in to such desires."

"Then let us be married tonight," she suggested, as if after all nothing could be more reasonable.

"Tonight?" He looked properly astonished. "You can't mean to elope," he continued. "Gretna is days from here, and our traveling alone together now would not be the least bit conducive to virtue, I'm afraid."

Margaret was enjoying her power to surprise him. "But I don't mean Gretna," she said, reaching into the pocket where she kept her father's remarkable gift. She unfolded the somewhat creased document and handed it to him. "With this we can be married in the village tonight," she concluded.

He took the paper from her, and reading it over, groaned. "Meg," he said, "think of the trouble and grief I have caused by acting impulsively—going to that masquerade, stealing the papers, kidnapping you. I promised myself I would yield to no more impulses if you would have me."

"I'm sorry to hear it," she said, but she smiled at him, and she could see he was confused and suspicious when she didn't try to press him further. She slipped the document into his coat pocket. "Ned says you always were a 'sudden' sort of person, and he did not think you would care to wait until the mourning period is over."

"What else did Ned tell you?" he asked, and Margaret felt an unworthy but entirely human satisfaction at the wariness in his tone. She would repay him a bit for all the times he had teased her. She did not answer.

Instead she asked, "Does my saying yes to your offer permit me to take liberties?"

She felt his fingers loosen in surprise when she spoke, so that she was able to close the distance between them and raise her hands to his face.

"Meg," he questioned, "what are you about?"

"Does my saying yes permit me to do this?" She touched his temples lightly, tracing the line of his brows, brushing his eyes closed with her fingertips, and outlining the bones of his cheeks. "And this?" she queried, stroking her thumbs across his lips. He stilled her hands, taking them into his own. His next words were strained and sad.

"Meg, I have no ring to give you. You have no luggage. If I take you to an inn tonight, you will be subject to the worst sort of conjecture and insult because of me." He paused. "As you were once before."

"I have your ring already, and we need not go to an inn."

"You are not suggesting a barn, I hope. I have too much to reproach myself with over the last barn we entered."

"There is Humphrey's cottage. You have a bed there." The hands holding hers were very strong. She had felt their strength often enough to rely on it entirely. Thus she could not miss the tremor that now shook them. He was resisting very hard, but he had not let go of her. She did not believe he wished to wait for their marriage any more than she did. And she believed his spirit, however chastened and subdued by loss and disgrace, was ever a bold one. There were things she had vowed to tell him to lessen his grief, but they could wait. Only one thing was needful now.

"I love you, Drew," she whispered. Then with a single swift motion he caught her about the waist and behind the knees and scooped her up in his arms to hold her against his heart. He strode to the window and stepped easily over the low sill out into the night.

"You do not need to carry me off this time," she protested as they crossed the wide lawn.

"But I do," he replied, "for Ned is holding Phantom for me in the wood." He grinned.

"Wretch," she cried. "You meant to elope all along." She squirmed lightly in his arms, and he stopped.

"No," he assured her solemnly, "I did not know you were here at Haddon, but I meant to ride to Wynrose tonight to find you, for I could not wait another day, Meg."

Margaret smiled, and though she could not know it, her smile was that particularly warm, shining sort of smile which expresses not mere gaiety but lasting joy. Her thief had not changed after all.

"I love you," she repeated, and this short, oft-repeated phrase delayed their elopement for some time as the Earl of Haddon's second son expressed himself in similar terms.

Avon Romances—
the best in exceptional authors and unforgettable novels!

HIGHLAND MOON   Judith E. French
76104-1/$4.50 US/$5.50 Can

SCOUNDREL'S CAPTIVE   JoAnn DeLazzari
76420-2/$4.50 US/$5.50 Can

FIRE LILY   Deborah Camp
76394-X/$4.50 US/$5.50 Can

SURRENDER IN SCARLET   Patricia Camden
76262-5/$4.50 US/$5.50 Can

TIGER DANCE   Jillian Hunter
76095-9/$4.50 US/$5.50 Can

LOVE ME WITH FURY   Cara Miles
76450-4/$4.50 US/$5.50 Can

DIAMONDS AND DREAMS   Rebecca Paisley
76564-0/$4.50 US/$5.50 Can

WILD CARD BRIDE   Joy Tucker
76445-8/$4.50 US/$5.50 Can

ROGUE'S MISTRESS   Eugenia Riley
76474-1/$4.50 US/$5.50 Can

CONQUEROR'S KISS   Hannah Howell
76503-9/$4.50 US/$5.50 Can